Souls Astray

a novel by Kellyn Roth

ISBN: 978-1-7341685-5-6

Cover design by Cover Culture
Interior design by Wild Blue Wonder Press

Kellyn Roth, Author
Wild Blue Wonder Press
3680 Browns Creek Road
The Dalles, OR, 97058
www.kellynrothauthor.com

WBW PRESS

For the lonely, the ashamed, the
misunderstood, and the ones to blame.

What if we could start over?

Part I: Adele

"I see how peoples are set against one another, and in silence, unknowingly, foolishly, obediently, innocently slay one another."

All Quiet on the Western Front by Erich Maria Remarque

Chapter One

April 1916
Kent, England

"Della-bell! Della-bell, where are you?" Kenneth's footsteps thudded heavily on the hallway as he searched. At seventeen, he was no longer stealthy, a fact for which Adele was eternally grateful. "Della-bell? There's been a letter."

Adele burst out of the closet. "A letter from Papa? But we had one yesterday!"

"Ha! Got you!" Kenneth's dark brown eyes, so like Adele's, danced. "Too gullible, little sister. I win."

Adele narrowed her eyes and launched herself at him. She wasn't sure if she was angry, exactly, but knew he must be punished. She jumped up, and he caught her and threw her into the air. "You *cheated*!" she exclaimed, wrapping her arms tight around his neck as he caught her back to him. "You didn't win; you didn't really find me!"

"I did, too!" Kenneth grinned broadly. "Just because you revealed yourself doesn't mean I didn't find you."

"But—"

"Oh, all right. Let's call this round of hide-and-seek a draw." Kenneth said, setting her on the ground. "I guess it was rather a dirty trick to play on my baby sister."

Adele stuck out her lip as far as it would go. "I'm not a baby. I'm seven."

Kenneth laughed. "Oh, right, I'd forgotten." He ruffled her hair, causing an already partially askew blue bow to dip below her ear. He awkwardly straightened it.

"What should we do next?" Adele fully intended to optimize every moment of Kenneth's time now that he was home from school for a few weeks. And, so far at least, her big brother hadn't complained, which was a special sort of wondrous.

"Oh, let's get outside while it's nice. You can't spend such a sunny day inside. Days like this are meant to be lived!"

They clattered down the broad front stairway and hurried out the door into the bright April sunshine.

"It's warm enough out that we don't need coats, but don't let Mother see us or she'd faint," he whispered, causing Adele to giggle.

"What shall we do?" she repeated when they were outside in the garden. "Not hide-and-seek again. You know all the good hiding places."

Kenneth chuckled. "I'm much bigger than you, Della-bell. You should be able to find me easily!

That's your advantage—but you still can't see what's right before your eyes."

Adele playfully punched his arm. "Come on. Let's go down by the brook."

Kenneth rolled his eyes up into his head. "You and that little stream. I guess you spend half your time there, don't you, Della-bell?"

"It's pretty!"

"And it makes Mother angry when you come home soaking wet, doesn't it, now?" Kenneth caught Adele and tickled her under the arms. "But that only sweetens the splashing."

Adele grinned. Mother was always trying to get her daughter to be a proper lady, but that wasn't easy—especially for a seven-year-old who liked to run and jump and play with boys, particularly Kenneth when he was home from school, and splash in wet, cold streams.

So, if she couldn't make Mother happy, why not have as much fun making her mad as possible?

"Well, you and Louis both make Mother so happy—especially Louis—that I shouldn't have to as well." She cocked her head. "Besides, she's just mad because I'm myself."

Kenneth shook his head in amusement. "Oh, Della-bell." He took her hand and followed her to the brook which was located over the hill.

Adele liked visiting the city, but her home was here in Kent on their little piece of property near the tiny village of Creling. She loved it here. After all, it had the prettiest brooks to splash in, the cheeriest village to visit, the best people … She didn't know why anyone would want to live anywhere else.

She let go of Kenneth's hand to run the rest of the way down to the brook. She heard his footsteps catching up with her in broad strides, but she arrived at the grassy bank, layered with daisies, before him.

Here the water trickled over a group of rocks in a gentle waterfall, all the pebbles looking colorful under the water. A group of trees shaded the area, and sunlight filtered through, green-tinted and lazy.

Her favorite parts of the scene, of course, were the cheerful little yellow and white flowers. Adele loved flowers more than anything. They were so pretty, so cheerful, so delicate. She knelt to collect a bouquet.

Kenneth arrived behind her. "This is one of the prettiest spots; you've got that much right. Does this section of the brook belong to us?"

Adele shrugged and rose, her floral treasures clutched in her fist. She didn't know. It could belong to their neighbors down the way, too, or to the biggest estate to the east where Uncle Caleb, one of her father's soldier friends, lived.

But she didn't care. No one had stopped her from playing there—and for a somewhat lonely seven-year-old who didn't have much of anyone to talk to outside of her family, a special spot was a necessity. Or at least it was convenient.

However, it didn't matter how special it was—she would always share everything with Kenneth. She didn't know what she'd do without him.

She gave her flowers to him to hold, and they strolled along the bank, pausing only to pick up pebbles to splash into the water with a satisfying *plop.*

"Papa and Louis will be here soon," Adele said, breaking the comfortable silence that had fallen between them.

"I know." Kenneth stared off up the creek, eyes half-shuttered. "Good to have them here at the same time as me, I guess."

Adele cocked her head. "You guess?"

"Yes. I guess." He ruffled her hair again, and she swatted his hand away.

"But why aren't you sure? Don't you want to see Louis and Papa?" she asked.

He sighed and ran a hand over his face. "Yes, Della-bell. I want to see Louis and Father. But at the same time, I don't." He cocked his head. "When I was in London with a few schoolmates, we met a group of women on the streets. They gave me this." Kenneth handed her the flowers again, reached into his well-cut jacket, and pulled something out of the inside pocket. He extended it to Adele.

Wonderingly, Adele accepted the object from her brother and twirled it in her fingers. "What is it?"

"A white feather."

"I know that." Adele laughed nervously. She sensed something strange in the air between them, something she couldn't quite pin down. "But why do you have it?" She hesitated. "Is it … a present for me?" Sometimes Kenneth brought her things home from London, but usually they made sense. Like a new doll or sweets or ribbons—one could never have enough ribbons.

He chuckled, the sound grinding on her ears oddly. "No, Della-bell. Not a present." He took the feather back from her and tucked it into his coat pocket again. "How old would you say I look, Della-bell?"

"You're seventeen." Honestly, Kenneth asked the silliest questions sometimes!

"No, but … what age do I *look* to you? Could I pass for eighteen? Nineteen? Twenty?"

Adele looked up at her big brother's frowning face, then regarded his long legs and broad shoulders. "Nineteen, but not twenty," she said at last.

"That's what they thought in London. That I was a man." He clenched his teeth. "And, really, seventeen is a man, I think."

She was cynical of this—though he was much older than she, he wasn't quite a man yet—and shrugged her shoulders. But if Kenneth said so.

"You see, Della-bell—" He patted his pocket, but his face quickly turned to a scowl. "Oh, never mind. Let's go back to the house." All the sunshine had gone out of his face and voice. Adele stepped to his side and took his hand, allowing her bouquet to fall to the ground unheeded.

"Are you all right, Kenny?"

"Yes, I'm quite all right." He sighed. "Come now. It's almost time for tea."

"No, it's not. It's hardly two."

"Well, anyway, I have some reading to do before the holiday's over."

Adele wrapped her fingers tighter around her brother's hand. "What is it, Kenny? Can you tell me? I can keep a secret. I promise."

Kenneth hesitated, staring at her face, then knelt in front of her and put his hands on her shoulders. "Della-bell, you know how the first thing Louis did when the war started was sign up?"

"Well, he was going to be in the army, anyway," Adele said. Like his father before him, Louis Collier was strictly military. Unlike her precious Kenneth. Kenneth was going to be something grand, she was sure—a doctor or lawyer or Prime Minister.

"Yes, but ..." Kenneth's words trailed off. "Della-bell, I want to join up."

Adele wrinkled her nose. "Join the war, you mean?" That didn't make sense. "I thought you were going to go to college."

"Yes, but ... everyone else ... everyone else is joining up. My older schoolmates are planning on it." He shrugged.

"But that doesn't mean you should." Something like panic tightened in Adele's chest. He couldn't join the army. He was her Kenneth. He belonged to her, and she couldn't let anyone who belonged to her go off to France where, well, anything could happen.

One couldn't live anywhere in England now and avoid hearing about someone's son or brother or husband dying. It was dangerous over there, and therefore not a place for Adele's big brother to go. Ever.

Louis and Papa were different. That was their job. Her father, Papa, had been going off to strange faraway places all her life, and Louis had started doing that, too.

But Kenneth was precious. Kenneth was hers. The only person who really belonged to Adele all the way. No one else loved her like Kenneth did.

"Yes, but …" Kenneth sighed. "I think it's rather my duty to join up."

"I don't think so. Besides, you can't until next year."

Kenneth's hand was in his pocket again. She knew he was fingering the feather. "I could forge documents. I was raised in a military home—I know what they will want from me and how to get it faked."

"But you could go to prison for that!" Adele exclaimed. "Besides, Mother wouldn't like it."

"Yes, she wouldn't like it. But if I were to do this, I'd be rather beyond what Mother would like." His hand dropped to his side. "I feel as if … as if I want to do something useful. Like Father and Louis."

Adele could understand feeling useless, but that wasn't any reason to run off and join the army. "But why?"

"Because … it's difficult to explain, Della-bell. You wouldn't understand."

Adele's brow wrinkled. "But I love you. I don't want you to get hurt."

Kenneth chuckled and squeezed her shoulder. "I love you, too. But I need to go. Can't you see? This would … this would make me as capable and strong and *brave* as Louis—or even Father. And that'd be … that'd be everything I ever wanted."

"But what about me?"

He grinned down at her. "What about you?"

"What … what will I do while you're gone?" she asked. She couldn't put it into words, quite, but Kenneth was her best friend. She loved her parents and Louis, but Kenneth was different. He was so important, so much a part of her life.

"What you do when I'm here, I imagine, only without me. You'll be fine." Kenneth turned back toward the house, and Adele followed him.

She didn't know what to say. Nor what she could do to deter him.

"You can be brave, too, Della-bell." A smile quirked about the edges of his lips. "You can keep the homefires burning."

Adele scowled. "I don't want to."

"Well, you've got to, so there you go." He glanced at her. "And, er, don't tell Mother."

"Why? What are you going to do?"

"Go a few towns over and join the army." He reached over and tugged at a lock of her hair. "Not until Father and Louis leave, though. So don't worry about that. I'll wait until they're gone to make my exit."

"All right," Adele said after a moment. "I won't tell Mother. But you have to promise to be very safe and come home."

"Of course, of course. How could I not when my Della-bell is waiting for me?" he teased.

Adele beamed. Kenneth didn't seem worried at all. Everything would be just fine.

Chapter Two

Adele raced out of the door and into her father's arms. He scooped her up and planted a scratchy, bearded kiss on both of her cheeks. He was wearing his fancy uniform and looked well in it, she thought—quite noble, as a father ought to look.

He set her down and moved past her to greet Mother. A quick peck to the cheek, brief as a kiss could be, and then he shook Kenneth's hand.

Louis touched her shoulder briefly as he stepped past her on the way to his mother, who he embraced before passing beyond her into the house.

Louis was like Papa in many ways. Strictly military. *Someday*, Adele thought, *he'll kiss his wife "hello" as if she were a distant cousin who he didn't care a bit about but was obligated to greet, and will probably treat his daughter like a silly creature who doesn't deserve to be listened to.*

But that was all right. She had Kenneth. Though Mother and Papa didn't like Kenneth, because he never obeyed them, Adele loved him most of all.

Adele and Kenneth followed their parents and

Louis into the parlor. Papa immediately took a seat on his chair next to the fireplace, and Mother lowered herself into the seat opposite him.

"Has everything been going well since I was here last?" Papa asked.

"Yes, of course. Nothing unusual." Mother inclined her head. "How are things at the front?"

"Oh, fine!" Papa reclined in his chair and crossed his legs at the ankle. "Just grand."

"That's good. I've heard the suffering is terrible in the trenches."

"It is, but nothing our boys can't handle."

Adele crawled into her father's lap. "When are you and Louis going back?" she asked.

"Soon. In a few days." He adjusted her so her head laid against his chest as he continued, "But I get to spend time with my Adele before then."

"So are things not as terrible as they say?" Mother asked. "Are things … are things going well? Will it be over soon, do you think?"

Papa's brow wrinkled for a second, then he smiled. "Oh, it'll be over by Christmas, I'm sure. I think we'll have a major breakthrough soon. That's why Louis and I were able to leave—the calm before the victory, this is."

"That's not what the papers hint at," Kenneth said from across the room where he sat in the corner. Kenneth tended to sit away from his parents and Louis, and even Adele, during family gatherings, though she was never quite sure why. "They do their best to keep up morale and all, but we're getting a beating, now, aren't we?"

"Don't talk back to me, Kenneth Collier," Papa snapped. "You're just a lazy schoolboy. When you work in a man's world, you can discuss these subjects with me. But for now, I'll take none of your mouth."

"But you don't want me to join up, now, do you?" Kenneth asked. "You just want me to stay home and be even more lazy."

"Going to college and getting yourself an education would most decidedly not be lazy," said Papa. "I want you to go to college and work hard—and when this war is over, which will be soon, you will be ahead of the rest who ran off and joined the army."

Kenneth's eyes flashed. "Isn't that what you did? What Louis did?"

"Yes, but unlike you, Louis—and I—are well fit for the army. Louis will rise in the ranks, as I have." Papa glared down at his youngest son. "You couldn't make a success of the military life if you wanted to."

Kenneth rose to his feet then sat down abruptly. "That's not true. How would you know that when you've never given me a chance? Why is Louis any better than me?"

"Because you're lazy. You're soft. You never tried hard for anything in your life. And perhaps that is partially my fault—and your mother's—but it is also part of your nature. Louis, however, can take a great deal more than you, and is therefore the son I would choose to be at my side during a battle."

Mother's eyes dropped, and Adele squirmed. Even Louis seemed uncomfortable with this statement, but he didn't speak up for Kenneth—and neither did Mother. Adele didn't know what to say. She knew Papa wouldn't particularly like any defense of Kenneth from her, but it didn't seem fair to not speak up.

"I love Kenneth," Adele said at last. Surely she wouldn't get in trouble for that.

"Mm, well, we all love Kenneth, of course, but that doesn't mean we approve of him." Papa shot one last sharp glance at his son then returned his eyes to his wife and began chatting with her about things Adele didn't care about—things that didn't matter.

Louis took part in the conversation. Kenneth didn't. He just sat there, eyes downcast. Once he glanced up, and she caught a glint in his eyes that she didn't particularly care for.

She guessed that Kenneth would be joining up—or trying to—sooner rather than later.

~

The days when the whole Collier family was safe at home were few and restless. Papa spent the entire time bragging on himself and Louis—as well as talking about how Britain would, could, must triumph in this war, and soon. He was all confidence, and Adele didn't have any reason not to believe him.

She hoped it would be over soon. Then Kenneth wouldn't run off and get himself hurt, and he'd become the man she hoped he would be—believed he should be—and knew he could be.

Then, one morning a few days after Papa and Louis left, Mother burst in Adele's bedroom before the sun had peaked the horizon.

Her skin was snow-white, and she had a white slip of paper clutched in her hand.

"Adele Elizabeth, did you know about this?" She dropped the slip of paper on Adele's pillow.

Adele picked it up and squinted at the words in the low light. She sounded out the words in Kenneth's tidy simple script one by one.

Dear Mother,

I have decided to join the army. I know neither you nor Father will be pleased with me, but it is a decision I have made for myself. I'll try to get in contact with you once I am safe in France where you can't stop me.

Tell Della-bell I'm being safe, just like I promised her. And don't you worry about me, either. I can handle the war just as well as, Louis or Father, if not better.

Your loving son,
Kenneth Judah Collier

"You knew."

Adele glanced up at her mother. "He … he said he wanted to join up, I guess."

Mother's eyes were full of cold fury. "Where has he gone?"

"I don't know."

A hard slap landed across Adele's cheek, and she cried out and clutched it.

"He's told you! He tells you everything."

"He told me he was going; that's all!" Adele pushed herself up and jumped out of the bed. "I don't know!"

Mother narrowed her eyes then snatched up the note and whirled out of the room. Adele followed her down the stairs to the foyer where their new telephone awaited her.

Mother had the war office on the phone in minutes, using her husband's name to get through. She asked that Kenneth Judah Collier be blocked from enlisting due to his age and lack of parental permission.

Part of Adele hoped her mother would be able to stop him—but another part of her didn't. She wanted more for Kenneth. More than her parents wanted him to have. She wanted him to be free to do what he wanted.

Really, wasn't that love? Craving the best for the person one cared about even if it was hard to give?

Besides, it would be glorious to have her favorite brother be a war hero. She just knew he'd do well and come back with a chest full of medals and then—then he'd show their parents.

If Kenneth could succeed at more than her parents thought he could, there was hope for her, too.

~

It was almost seven weeks later when Adele heard from Kenneth for the first time.

Dear Della-bell,

I've recently arrived in France.

There is a forest—but not one like we have at home. There aren't nearly so many pretty brooks. Make sure you go visit ours sometimes.

I haven't seen the Eiffel Tower or the Arc de Triomphe yet, but we have plans to march there someday.

The scenery isn't quite what we imagined when we talked about visiting France in the past, but don't worry. There's a lovely breeze from the south this evening, and the sunset was nice enough.

Not much going on here to mention. Busy, not much time to write, but just day-to-day routine. Tell Mother it's not so bad. No fuss required.

I look forward to receiving your letter; and yes, you must write me one. I think that falls under the umbrella of sisterly duties. Have Mother help you with the spellings a bit. Hard to make out your chicken scratch, Della-bell, when you wrote me at school, and I don't have time to make it out now.

Will try to bring you a souvenir, yes, yes. I'm not sure what that present will be, but maybe I'll think of something before the war's over. Or else I'll take you to France, and we'll see it together.

With love,
Kenneth

His words reassured her worried heart, and she felt confident that nothing would go poorly with him. He would be all right. He'd come home to her.

She had to make herself believe that as she'd made herself believe it for her father and Louis. She would will them to come home. She'd will the bullets away with prayers and wishes and every breath. Because she couldn't let such a thing happen to her family as it did to the crumbling homes around her.

Mother's eyes grew worried as she read Kenneth's letter. Adele wondered why, but her mother didn't say.

"At least he was safe when he wrote this," she said softly as she folded the letter and slid it back into its envelope.

Adele accepted the missive from her mother. "Is he safe now?"

"I don't know. I pray that he is. I pray that he gets over this and comes home to us." Mother ran a hand over her forehead then turned to go to her room. She'd been staying in there an awful lot now.

"Will praying help?" Adele asked.

Mother paused and glanced over her shoulder at her daughter. "Yes. Of course. Of course it will."

"Then I'll pray," said Adele.

She did, out by the brook on the grassy bank, with her face buried in her knees and her eyes closed tight. That somehow, against all odds, all three of the men she loved would come home to her and be her beloved father and brothers again, and everything would turn out all right.

With a deep conviction, she believed that because she'd prayed it, it would happen. Praying meant God had heard her, and that meant that He must do what she asked. He was good, or so she'd been told. A good God would get her father and brothers safely home.

Chapter Three

The doorbell rang. Adele, lying on the floor of the parlor on a rainy midsummer day, propped herself up on her elbow, and the picture book slid away unheeded. Who would be coming to call on such a stormy day?

Mother appeared in the hallway. They'd let their one maid go recently when she'd married and had yet to find a new one—but Mother didn't seem to mind the work terribly, especially when it was just Adele tracking in mud and eating food.

"Now who could that be?" Mother's rhetorical question was expected and comforting. Adele closed her book and went to set in on the bookshelf.

The door clicked open. A postman stood behind it, eyes sad as he extended an envelope.

"Th-thank you." Mother accepted the slip of paper and turned it over in her hands. She didn't say a word to the messenger. She just stared at the missive silently.

"What is it?" Adele asked. She drew close to her

mother and placed a hand on her arm. Mother let her arms drop slightly under the weight of her daughter's touch. "What is it? Will you open it now?"

Mother shook her head slowly. "Could be anything, I suppose," she said in a hoarse whisper. "Even if it's bad news, it could be notice of injury … or missing in action. Even that would be … would be better. Less final, you know."

"Have you anyone with you, Elizabeth?"

She shook her head.

"She has me," Adele said stoutly.

The man gave her a condescending smile then moved his eyes back to her mother. "Who could I call for you?"

"I have friends," she said, "but I can call them myself."

"All right, then. I'll leave you, unless you think there'll be a return note."

Her head moved to indicate the negative.

"Very well. I hope for your sake that it's good news—or at least not the worst." The man tipped his cap and ventured back out into the rain.

The door eased shut. Mother stepped into the parlor, still regarding the yellow scrap of paper like it held the power of life and death to her.

It couldn't, of course. It was just a scrap of paper. But something told Adele not to say anything more. To keep her mouth shut and worriedly watch her mother's face for any sign of what was going on.

"I should just get it over with. I've expected it, after all. I'm a military wife. I knew the risks when I married the man …" Her voice trailed off. "But I didn't know about this terrible war. And I didn't know that our son would join up. Two … two of my sons. Oh, God, why didn't you give me daughters?"

"I'm a daughter," Adele observed. "What does the letter say?"

"I haven't opened it. You can see that." Her words weren't harsh or condescending. She stated it as fact. It was as if, in that moment, the proper, cold marble had been stricken from Mother, leaving her soft and pale and frightened. "I … I didn't realize that the hardest thing would be forcing myself to learn the truth."

Adele wondered if her mother even remembered she was in the room. She seemed to be talking to herself, or to the letter, or something of the sort. But definitely not to Adele.

"Let me." Adele took the envelope from her mother and quickly tore it. She pulled the paper out and unfolded it.

She stared at the neat, formal typewriter print with narrowed eyes. "We regret to inform you …" she sounded out.

Mother ripped the telegram from her daughter's fingers. Adele could almost see her mother force herself to read the words, to form them into meaningful sentences in her mind. Then the paper floated to the floor.

Everything in Adele was cold and empty and lifeless. She didn't know what to think of this extreme feeling of empty apathy. It was as if her will to understand what was happening at this present moment had been revoked. She was nothing, the words on the telegram were nothing, and the look on her mother's face was nothing.

Mother crumpled into herself. She fell to the floor, clutched her legs to her chest, and buried her face in her knees. Adele stood there for a moment, not knowing what to do.

Could that be her mother, curled up on the floor sobbing softly? Mother always liked to keep her gowns clean. Mother hated dirt and dust, which was abundant on the ground. Mother hated shows of emotions. Mother hated exactly what she was doing now.

"Mother?" Adele said the moniker three times but received no acknowledgement. She picked up the scrap of paper now, the scrap of paper which held the power to change her mother until she was nothing but a pitiful creature weeping on the floor.

We regret to inform you that Colonel Louis Collier and Lieutenant Louis E. Collier were killed in action ...

Adele read the words over and over again, trying to comprehend them. This didn't mean that … that her darling papa and her brother Louis were gone, did it? They'd be coming back, wouldn't they?

She glanced at her mother, still huddled on the floor, then back to the paper in her hand. At last, she walked quietly into the foyer and lifted the receiver from its cradle. After a few minutes of discovering how to speak with an operator, she reached one of her mother's many friends.

"Hello, it's me," she said in a very small voice.

"Why, hello, Adele."

She breathed a sigh of relief. Her mother's friend recognized her voice. That was something. "My … my papa died. And Louis. Could you come take care of my mother?"

There was silence on the line for a long time, and Adele wondered if the connection had gotten cut off due to the storm. Tears threatened. She forced them back, swallowed, spoke again.

"Are you still there?"

"Y-yes. I'll be right over. You stay right where you are, sweetling."

Adele clinked the receiver back where it belonged and glanced back into the parlor from where she stood. Her mother still hadn't moved.

Would she ever come back?

~

Two weeks later, not much about Mother had changed. She'd gotten off the parlor floor and been half carried to her bedroom when a group of friends had arrived, but since then, she'd barely stirred from her chair by the window.

There she sat, eyes glazed over, an odd burning light in them. Her face was like ice or stone. Empty, emotionless. Just then, Adele would have done anything to make her mother feel an emotion—anger, hatred, disgust. But though she came into her mother's bedroom and said her silliest things and bothered her half to death, she got no response. She almost wished her mother would begin crying again. But Mother didn't.

Adele wasn't crying, either. She wasn't sure why,

really. She ought to cry. People ought to cry when their papa and big brother die. But she felt numb. Like she wasn't even sure they were gone—not really. It seemed so unreal, so distant from her, like any day now they'd receive notice that it was all a lie and her father and brother would be coming back some day, like they always did.

People came over and wandered in and out of the house at all hours. Friends, relatives, neighbors … all offering their condolences. Oftentimes they'd bring a pie or some sweets or flowers.

Mother didn't notice. Adele enjoyed them, but she wasn't sure if she ought to be enjoying anything just then, so there was a taste of guilt in the pie and sweets and the scent of betrayal in the flowers.

Flowers shouldn't be used as a way to mourn, anyway. They were too happy. Flowers and sadness just didn't go together.

They hadn't heard from Kenneth recently and weren't even sure that he'd gotten notice of his father and brother's death. Adele hoped he would hear on a day when he could bear it. There were good days and bad days, and one hoped for an inbetweenish day to hear the worst of news. A good day would be ruined, a bad day would break your heart all the more, but an inbetweenish day was much better.

Adele had heard about it on an inbetweenish day. Perhaps her mother had been having a good day or a bad day when she heard, though, and that was why she was so unable to cope.

Disloyal as it was, Adele wasn't quite sure why Mother had reacted so violently. She didn't think her family loved each other very much. They seemed to be very casual and unemotional about it, at least. But she supposed anyone ought to be as sad as Mother—and that was why it was odd that she herself couldn't feel a thing.

She ought to be sad. She ought to sit in her room and stare out the window and be unable to handle all the emotions in her breast, to give up and just feel nothing at all.

But that wasn't how Adele felt at all. She felt odd, she felt disbelieving, but she didn't feel sad or unable to handle the news. Even if it were true and Papa and Louis were dead, well, she supposed she'd bear up, somehow.

Still, it didn't feel like it was really happening.

Without her mother's support, though, Adele wasn't sure what to do. But, she remembered eventually, she wasn't alone. At least, she wasn't as alone as she felt.

She had Kenneth. Her darling, handsome, wonderful, strong, smart brother Kenneth. So ever in her heart sang the refrain:

Kenneth will be home soon. He promised me he'd be home soon. He seems to think everything is all right. He'll live. He'll come back to us. He's got to. He'll take care of me, and Mother, and everything will be all right no matter what.

She had to believe it. Had to believe that Kenneth would be her savior in the end. That someday he'd be home, someday he'd take care of things, someday he'd be there to love and spoil and bring her gifts and tell her she was beautiful and special and worthy.

With Kenneth, she could be brave, because Kenneth was so brave. She didn't know how to be brave without him. But with? That would be as easy and natural as breathing.

~

A week had passed when Mother rose from her chair and walked out of her room. She went to the bathroom, washed her face, dried it with a cloth, then stared at her reflection in the mirror for a good two minutes.

Afterward, she walked downstairs to the telephone and made a series of calls to a variety of people either informing them of the death of her loved ones, making arrangements for memorial services, or taking care of the business end of death, morbid as that was.

Adele watched with a tight throat and cramped stomach. But this was better than before, wasn't it? Her mother still hadn't spoken to her, still wasn't cheerful, still hadn't cried more, still hadn't gotten angry … but walking was better than sitting, and making phone calls even better than not talking at all.

At last Adele got up the courage to approach Mother between calls.

"Mother?" she said in a small voice.

Mother pinioned her daughter with her eyes, cold and lifeless. "Yes, Adele?"

"Are you … are you all right?"

Mother blinked. "My husband and son have been brutally killed. So, no, I am not all right. I shall be in time, but I am not at present."

Adele nodded jerkily.

"In fact, I find it odd that my only daughter, who was so beloved by her father and her older brother, could be so cold in the face of their death." Tears welled in Mother's eyes, but she dashed them away. "It's as if you have no feeling. You're seven years old. You should be frightened and grieved. You shouldn't be going about as if nothing has happened and cutting capers and pretending I'm the one who needs to behave myself."

Adele knew this was true, but she didn't hang her head. She just stared at her mother blankly for a time before she answered. "I don't know why I'm not sad. I suppose it's because I know Kenneth will come home and take care of us." *He makes me brave. He makes me able to bear this.* But she couldn't put that into words she could say out loud, so she just said: "I love him best, you know."

Mother's face contorted with pain for a second, then she forced it to smooth out to recognizable features. "I see. So you're a selfish, unfeeling child. How I brought such a wicked little demon into the world is beyond me."

It was hard to be seven when one didn't understand that words spoken in grief and anger and fear are not words that are meant.

Adele left the room and went to her bedroom, and she did cry, by herself, as wicked, unfeeling, selfish demons are known to do.

Chapter Four

"But when can Kenneth come home, Uncle Caleb?" Adele asked for the fifth time that day. She stamped her foot with frustration. She really must know.

"After the war, dear," said Uncle Caleb. He was one of Papa's army buddies—only he was a Major General. That meant he could come home to help Mother sort through the legalities of dying.

Funny how someone dying meant that one spent ages working on trying to get money transferred and all other sorts of things that really didn't matter, that one really didn't care about because a dear person was gone.

But one had to. One had to make sure everything was all right. That the will reading was done, and the money was transferred, and the property still belonged to the right person, and on and on. It was all people ever talked about anymore.

She only hoped Kenneth would come home soon. She loved him so much, and she knew he would make everything better. He just had to.

Uncle Caleb picked up the receiver of the telephone and got through to the War Department even easier than Mother had.

"Ask about Kenneth," Adele whispered, tugging on his arm.

He brushed her away. "Shush!" Then, "No, not you. I have my adopted niece here, and she's driving me bonkers."

Adele scowled. She wasn't driving Uncle Caleb bonkers. All she wanted was one simple thing, and he could do it if he wanted to. She knew very well that he could. He was just being stubborn.

"Just ask about Kenneth," she repeated. She hadn't heard a thing from him in weeks, and though in the army that could mean anything, she wanted to know now. And if one had a Major General as an uncle, one might as well use him for something.

"While I have you, can you look up, er, let me think, Kenneth Judah Collier? He's probably a private —enlisted earlier this spring, April I think, and he's in France somewhere … Yes, I can wait. Why don't you ring me up when you find out?"

Adele squealed. Uncle Caleb shushed her but smiled.

"I just want to know his whereabouts, et cetera. Nothing fancy. Whatever you can find, though. His little sister wants to know if he's safe or not. Right. Right, thank you." He gave the clerk the number he was calling from and hung up the receiver.

"There. Are you satisfied, you little pest?" he asked.

Adele gave Uncle Caleb a big hug. "Thank you, thank you, thank you! Do you think he's all right?"

"I couldn't tell you, Adele." He sobered. "There are so many young men losing their lives out there. I have no reason to believe that Kenneth is one of them. It takes months for mail to get sorted a lot of the time, and if he's not writing to you, that's probably because he's busier. Don't worry about it."

Adele had been trying not to worry, but it was terribly difficult. She wanted Kenneth here now—and yet it seemed like the war might be going on for years and years more.

Uncle Caleb wasn't quite as optimistic as Papa had been—or perhaps he was more honest.

It was only a few hours later when the telephone rang. Uncle Caleb answered it.

Adele rushed over to his side, attempting to hear something of what the man on the other end of the phone line was saying, but she couldn't.

She only had the expression on his face and his brief responses to go off of.

His brow was wrinkled, his blue eyes dark. He ran his hand through graying brown hair and sighed.

"Yes, yes, I see. Well, be sure to call as soon as you find out more. Do me a favor—keep an eye on the situation. I'm with the mother and her family for at least a few more days. Of course. I'm quite thankful for you taking the time. I know how busy you are …"

At last he got off the phone. His shoulders sloped as he turned to Adele. "Let's go into the parlor and talk," he said, attempting a smile.

Adele felt like crying or screaming, but she

didn't. She just quietly followed Uncle Caleb into the parlor. He took a seat on the sofa and pulled her down into his lap.

"Now understand that it's difficult to know anything for sure," he said to start, "but the clerk told me that Kenneth was recently declared missing in action. This is new information, so they hope he'll turn up soon. It has happened before. The army makes mistakes, people are lost in the crowd, and he could be safely tucked away somewhere regardless. But they believe he may be among the dead. There was a big battle, and there's a lot of sorting to do."

Adele narrowed her eyes. "But he's not dead?"

"No. At least, we don't know that he's dead yet." Uncle Caleb took a deep breath. "But Adele, you must understand that they're not optimistic. They believe he must be among the dead—or the wounded, but that's a fragile hope. It's just … sometimes when so many men die at once, it can be hard to keep track of them."

Adele swallowed. She'd been raised on terrible tales of battles and death and man's cruelty—Papa felt that telling his sons such things would make them tougher, and Kenneth had loved to frighten her with them—but it was more terrible this time.

Because it could be Kenneth lying in a pile of bodies, drenched in his own blood.

He could be dead. She might never see him again.

Adele swallowed hard then shook her head.

She couldn't let herself focus on that terrible possibility. She had to focus rather on the hope that Kenneth could be alive. That he might be among the wounded or perhaps someone had made a mistake.

Uncle Caleb held her against his broad chest for a long time before he stood, setting her on her feet, and walked out of the room to the foyer. "I'm going to tell your mother what we know."

Adele watched Uncle Caleb walk slowly up the stairs. He wasn't much older than her father, and she knew he still led the occasional charge on the battlefield. However, she'd never seen his steps so slow, his shoulders so sloped.

She supposed it must be difficult to have to deliver such bad news so many times. She knew they weren't the only family he'd visited. He'd come straight from his sister's house. His nephew had been lost—and his brother—and oh so many others.

Friends, family, dear ones, even people one didn't care about a great deal … it all hurt. Because death, especially such cruel death, was so wrong.

So unnatural.

So scary.

After a bit, she followed Uncle Caleb up the stairs. Her mother was standing by the window in her bedroom. Uncle Caleb stood near the doorway, so Adele had to peek around him to see Mother.

"Will you be all right?" he asked.

"Y—yes. I mean … I'll be all right. I … I suppose we can't know anything certainly for a time."

Uncle Caleb shook his head. "No. But you realize the chances are …"

"Yes. I realize." She glanced over her shoulder. Tears glistened in her eyes. "I realized it, of course, when I married an army man. I realized that I shouldn't count on tomorrow, that anything could happen. But of course … of course I always hoped —" She paused and pressed her hand to her mouth. "Could you leave me for a bit?"

"I understand." He sighed. "Times like these I wish I could have remained single. There's such risk in it."

Mother bit her bottom lip. "We looked at the risks and thought it would be all right. And then, so late on … I didn't expect it. I thought when he was considering leaving the army a few years ago that it was over, and I didn't need to worry about him anymore. That I could stop laying in my bed alone at night and wondering if he was fighting his last battle, if I would ever see him again … if his last visit truly had been the last. Then this war began, and Louis joined, and now Kenneth … Oh, God, where is Your love in this?"

Uncle Caleb took a step forward and then paused. "I don't have an answer for that. I imagine someday I'll get to Heaven, and it will all make perfect sense. For now, I can only cling to the belief that He is loving, and He does have a purpose for the pain. That He wouldn't lie. That all the sin this world has fallen in will be wiped away, and Heaven will be better than anything I can imagine."

"Patience is a virtue." Mother laughed brokenly. "Will they phone when they know more?"

"Yes. I'll … I'll stay and wait for it. Ella won't mind; she can't leave her sister, but she wants me to be here. Could be days, but I imagine they'll know more by this evening. At least I rather hope so."

Mother nodded. Uncle Caleb turned and left the room, almost bumping into Adele in the process. He glanced down at her, then nodded toward her mother before proceeding down the stairs.

Adele slowly crept into her mother's bedroom.

"M—Mama?" It had been years since she'd called her mother anything but "Mother." But for some reason, "Mama" was more appropriate in that moment. It burst from Adele's lips before she could think about it.

"Adele." Mother moved to her seat beside the window again, sinking into it and clinging to the arms like her very being depended on the seat for support. Probably it did.

"Mama, do you think Kenny is all right? Mama—Mama, do you think so? I'm so … I'm so afraid. What if Kenny is dead? What will we do? Where will we go? Mama …" Adele stumbled across the room and placed her hands on the arms of the chair. Her mother looked up at her blankly.

"So. It's Kenneth you care about, is it?" Mother returned her eyes to the landscape outside. "Hmm."

"Of course I care about Kenny!" Adele reached up to dash the nasty hot tears from her eyes.

The growing panic, the fury, the disbelief, the grief—it was all too much for her.

But Mama … Mama could make it better.

If only she would hold Adele a little and tell her it would be all right.

"But not your father or Louis. Interesting." Mother looked Adele in the eyes then. "You're such a little brat. If I weren't a lady, I'd use a stronger word for you, young woman. You only care about the people who are willing to make your life easy and treat you like a princess and never go against you—even if what we want is what's best for you."

Adele stepped back, shocked. "But … but … Kenny, Mama!"

"No. I don't care. You're so selfish, so unfeeling." Mother arose abruptly and brushed past her daughter to her vanity.

With one arm, she swept Kenneth and Adele's portraits off the surface.

They landed on the floor with a crash. Glass shattered, wood cracked.

Adele stared blankly at the feathering of cracked glass obscuring her smiling face of a few years ago, the broken frame of Kenneth's.

Mother regarded the shattered picture frames in blank confusion, as if she didn't understand her own actions. A low moan escaped Adele's lips at last, and she ran out of the room.

The phone rang. The worst happened.

Neither Adele nor Mother spoke to each other for the rest of day.

Chapter Five

October 1916

Adele walked slowly down the path toward the village of Creling, scuffing up piles of golden and red leaves with her toes. Her mother had sent her in with a pocket of money and a list to buy some small grocery items. Mother rarely left her house anymore, and more often than not, shopping fell to Adele's lot.

She didn't mind shopping, really—just shopping for her mother.

She looked up from the small piles of leaves she accumulated in front of her shoes, and her eyes met another set, blinking at her. Only this girl's eyes were blue and fringed with almost transparent lashes while Adele's were brown and dark-rimmed.

"Hello," said Adele. "Who are you?"

The girl blinked rapidly. "I'm not supposed to speak with strangers," she said. "My mama would be mad."

Adele cocked her head. “Well, you spoke already.”

The girl clapped a hand over her mouth. “I’m so sorry!”

“Well, I don’t care,” said Adele, “and your mama isn’t here. I don’t think she’ll know.”

Another girl, like the first but smaller, came up followed by a pudgy baby of two or three. “Millie, who’s that?” the second girl asked, her golden curls bouncing about her rosy cheeks.

“I don’t know.” Millie looked Adele up and down. “Who are you?”

“I’m Adcle Collier.”

“Oh. Well, I’m Millie. Millie Lark. And these are my baby sisters, Ruthie and Shellie.”

“I’m not a baby!” Ruthie stamped her foot at the indignity of it.

Both the older girls ignored this.

“Well, now that we’ve been introduced, I suppose we can talk.” Adele offered half a grin. “Where are you from? I live in that house up the way.”

“I live in the cottage down the way.” Millie smiled. “My papa owns a shop in the town.”

“Oh? Which shop?” Adele asked.

“Lark’s,” said Millie.

“That’s where I’m going,” said Adele. She reached into her pocket. “I have to get these things for Mother.”

Millie accepted the paper and glanced down the list. “I can help you. I know where they all are.”

“I’d like that,” said Adele.

They started off down the road, Ruthie and Shellie trailing behind them.

“Do you have little sisters?” Millie glanced over her shoulder as she spoke, forehead wrinkled with annoyance.

“No,” said Adele. “I don’t want any, either. I … I used to have two big brothers, but now they’re both dead.” She swallowed.

“Oh, no! What happened?” Millie asked.

“The war,” Adele said. She didn’t want to go into any more details, but everyone in England understood just then. “My papa, too. He was a colonel.”

“I’m sorry. My papa has a bad leg, and he can’t join up. And I haven’t got any brothers—just Ruthie and Shellie.” She cocked her head. “I have an uncle in the army, though. We pray for him every night.”

Adele sighed. Everyone had an uncle or a friend or someone. It seemed like every family in the world was affected by this war in a terrible way.

“Mama says that even though we pray, we might have to wait until we get to Heaven to see Uncle Erwin again.” Millie smiled sadly. “But at least there’s Heaven! That’s a long ways away, but you’ll get to see your brothers and papa again.”

Adele blinked. She’d heard that, but somehow it was different coming from a stranger instead of a well-meaning relative, friend, or visitor. She wasn’t too sure she was going to Heaven. After all, Mother said she was a demon, and Adele was sure she must be right.

Mother would do many things, but lying wasn’t one of them. She was honest, even if she was sometimes rather mean. At least, Adele didn’t think other people called their daughters selfish demons.

“I suppose so,” she said doubtfully. “I don’t know

that I'm going to Heaven."

"Really? I am," said Millie. "Why do you think you're not?"

"I'm … I'm not sure I'm good enough."

Millie laughed. "Oh, I wouldn't worry about that. You just have to love God."

Love God. Hmm. She wasn't sure how she could do that, since God wasn't someone she could hug or kiss or talk to, but it was a thought. Especially since the alternative to Heaven was rather unappealing, and she'd like to see Kenneth again.

"What's Millie short for? Mildred?" Adele asked.

Millie shook her head emphatically. "Everyone always asks that, but it's not! It's Camilla."

"Ah. I'm Adele Elizabeth," Adele said. "What about you? If you have a longer one, I mean."

"Camilla Faith," Millie said. "And then Ruth Elise and Michelle Grace."

"Those are all pretty," said Adele.

They walked the rest of the way to the store chatting cheerfully together.

Now that she knew who Mr. Lark was—Millie's papa, that is—she rather liked him. He was cheerful and a good father.

He picked Shellie up and set her on the counter and chatted with Adele and Millie the whole time they searched for the proper items. He was slightly overweight and happy, and he teased and joked constantly. It was plain that Millie adored him.

Adele wished her father had been like that. It would have been so nice. But now he never would be like that. Her chest clamped oddly at the realization.

Oh, well. She supposed fathers weren't important anyway.

~

A few days later, Adele walked down to see Millie. She hoped they'd be able to spend the afternoon together. She wanted a friend, and somewhere to escape to, and the Larks' cottage provided her with both.

She found Millie curled up by the gate, crying softly.

"Millie! What is it?" Adele asked. She rushed over and wrapped her arms around her friend. "Can you tell me?"

Millie nodded shakily. "My … my uncle Erwin was killed. He … he was my favorite, and I loved him, and my mama … mama can't stop crying, and my papa looks so sad, and I just … I just don't know what I can do!"

Adele brought Millie's forehead down on her shoulder. "There, there. It's all right. It's all going to be all right. Don't worry. You'll … you'll see him in Heaven, right? That's what you told me. You'll see him in Heaven." Millie was going to Heaven, so that was a sure thing. She decided casting doubts on Uncle Erwin's final destination was a bad idea at this point.

"Yes, I will." Millie clung to Adele. "But … but it's so sad. I … I'm afraid my mama will just get sadder and sadder …"

"I know, I know. It's all right, Millie. I'm here for you."

All the things I wish someone would say to me. That's what will help, Adele thought as she rubbed small circles on Millie's back.

"I'll never see him again," Millie said. "Not on earth."

"I know. It's sad."

"It's very sad." Millie wiped her wet face with her sleeve. "I'm sorry. I didn't mean to be sad all over your sweater. Now it's all teary."

Adele glanced down at the wet patch on her front. "That's all right. I don't mind. It'll wash right out, I'm sure—and even if it doesn't, I don't care."

Millie took Adele's hand and squeezed it. "Thank you, Adele."

"You're welcome, Millie." Adele smiled. "Now, let's get inside! It's cold and looks like rain. You know what I think?"

"What?" Millie asked. She stood and wiped her face one last time, regarding Adele curiously.

Adele also stood and brushed away dead leaves that clung to the skirt of her dress. "I think your mama probably wants you to give her a hug and tell her everything will be all right. Same as I did for you. I think you can make her feel better."

Millie blinked rapidly. "Really?"

"Yes, really." Adele knew this because she had thought perhaps she could make her mother feel better, and in the very deepest part of her she believed that Louis would have been able to comfort Mother—if he wasn't dead, that was.

Unfortunately, Mother didn't want Adele to help—a selfish unfeeling demon. Nothing *she* did would make Mother feel better.

But Mrs. Lark—well, that was a different thing entirely. Mrs. Lark was a kind-faced, gentle woman, and she loved all three of her daughters devotedly.

Millie—as well as Ruthie and Shellie—would be able to make Mrs. Lark feel better. And, in return, Mrs. Lark would comfort them. Adele was only glad she got to tell her friend this, and to offer Millie herself a little comfort.

No one had been there for Adele—and perhaps she deserved it. She wasn't really worthy of notice. But Millie was a little angel, from the tips of her toes to the top of her blonde, ringlet-covered head. Millie deserved every ounce of comfort someone could give her.

Adele followed Millie into the house, spoke softly to the teary-eyed Mrs. Lark who smiled in spite of herself and gave Adele a big hug, smothered her against her ample bosom for a moment.

Adele appreciated the affection. It had been a long time since a grownup woman had touched her. For some reason mothers were infinitely more comforting than children or even men. She wasn't sure why, but that was how it was.

Even before Papa and Louis and Kenneth died, Mother hadn't touched Adele often. Now … now it was as if she didn't even know Adele was her daughter.

Didn't know that sometimes she just needed a hug.

Didn't know that if Mother would just try, just try a little, Adele would break down in her arms and sob until she couldn't breathe, until every bit of the anger and grief was rung out of her.

Soon she left the Larks behind, knowing they'd want each other during a time of grief, not a lonely little girl.

She walked all the way to her brook and sat in the damp, leaf-covered grass with her knees pulled up to her chest. Then she did cry, softly. She fought an inner battle that left her exhausted, but it brought her to a conclusion.

She could never trust anyone.

She could never rely on another person for her joy.

She could never tell her mother if she felt sad or happy.

She had to count on herself for every bit of safety and pleasure she squeezed out of life.

She'd never have a real family.

She had to determine her own future.

From now on, it was Adele for Adele.

Part II: Troy

"Burdens are for shoulders strong enough to carry them."

Gone with the Wind by Margaret Mitchell

Chapter One

London, England
Spring 1917

It was far too early in the morning for anyone to be tumbling out of bed. At least, that was what ten-year-old Troy Kee thought when his mother shook his shoulder and whispered, "*Bonjour*, Troy."

Good morning, indeed. It was hardly seven, and a growing boy needed his sleep!

But he forced himself to smile sleepily and whisper, "*Bonjour, Maman.*"

Maman walked across the room to his younger sister's bed and placed a gentle hand on the sleeping girl's shoulder. "*Bonjour*, Eloise."

Lola, age six, was up almost before her mother said the words.

Maman rarely used her daughter's effervescent nickname, unlike her husband and son who both thought it was preferable to three syllables, pronounced in the French fashion.

"*Bonjour, Maman.*" Lola hopped out of bed, dragging two dolls and a stuffed animal or three with her. "Is it sunshine-y?"

Maman laughed softly. "*Oui. Très* sunshine-y." She smoothed a hand over her daughter's strawberry-blonde locks, similar to her own in color, then turned to leave the room. "Both of you in the kitchen in half an hour, *comprenez vous*?"

"*Je comprends*," Troy mumbled, attempting to wipe the sleep from his eyes with both fists. Why was his mother such an early riser—and why did she insist that he should be one, too? He was always so sleepy in the mornings.

Lola bounced about cheerfully, collecting her clothes and then running off to the bathroom to change.

Troy slogged out of bed and found his trousers and shirt. He supposed he'd better get his messy reddish hair to lay down a bit. It wasn't as messy as Lola's was in the mornings, but it was sticking up some places and lying down oddly in others.

Eventually Troy made his way to the little kitchen at the front of their small home. His father sat at the table with a newspaper, a cup of tea, and a pipe, the model of British manhood, while his mother still wore her dressing gown and slippers and sipped coffee.

Troy could understand that; he preferred coffee to tea, too. He had his Britishisms, but tea just wasn't one of them. Couldn't stand it.

Of course, he wasn't generally allowed to have coffee, either.

He pulled back a chair at the little table in the kitchen and sat down next to Lola, who beamed at him before returning to her toast. Lola was such a happy girl. Even at 7:30 in the morning.

Troy was happy, too. Just not before eight.

"Have you heard from Henri recently, dear?" Papa asked without glancing up from his newspaper. Troy knew who his father was talking to, though. He always called Maman "dear," Troy "son," and Lola "sweetheart."

With Maman, it was harder to figure out. She called practically everyone *chéri*. That included strangers on the street at times. She was bubbly and joyful—*très charmant*.

He didn't know if that was because she was French or because she was his darling Maman, but whatever the reason, she was always happy.

Troy wanted to be like her in that, and he also wanted to be sensible and strong like his father. That wasn't too much to ask, really, was it?

"*Non*. Not recently, at least. But I like to believe he's safe, despite this horrible war." Maman's French accent made every word sharper when she was annoyed with something, and she was annoyed with the war. Troy understood that. It did seem to be causing a great deal of havoc.

"I'm sure he's quite well." Papa smiled at his wife and patted her hand where it rested on the table.

Her lips quirked up. "*Oui*. Or at least he's in God's hands. *Dieu le gardera*."

Papa nodded and returned to his newspaper for a second. Then he flipped it down and smiled at

Troy and Lola across the table.

"I forgot to say good morning to two of my three favorite people in this world."

Lola dashed about the table to give her father a kiss and a hug. Troy wasn't big on kissing at this point, but he rose and gave Papa a somewhat stiff embrace. He patted Troy's back and let him go. Papa was marvelously understanding about loving without physical affection.

"Do I get a good morning kiss?" Maman asked, faking a pout.

"You've had enough kisses this morning, I think, dear," Papa said from behind his newspaper.

Maman made a strangled laughing sound, and Troy glared. If he didn't want to hug or kiss his father, he absolutely didn't want to know that his parents were hugging or kissing. Ever.

"I don't think you can ever have enough kisses," Lola said. "That'd be like having enough happiness or enough … enough sweets."

Troy had to smile at that. It was like Lola to think one could never have enough sweets. He agreed, a bit, though. Chocolate was just about the best thing in the world.

"I'm afraid enough sweets is a definite possibility, Lola," said Papa, smiling at his daughter. "But you're right. Never enough kisses or happiness."

Kisses, indeed, thought Troy. *What earthly good are kisses?*

"*Chéri*, what time do you need to be at work today?" Maman asked. "We've the financials to go over, and you know I'm hopeless at that."

He frowned. “Oh, I can’t do that this morning. I really need to be off in a few minutes here. This evening?”

“*Bien, bien*. As long as one of us remembers.” Maman twirled a spoon around in her coffee as cream turned the dark brown to a light tan. “Only there’s Troy’s mathematics, too.”

“Mm. We’ll have to do that tonight, too.” Papa stood. “And I’m sure Henri will write soon; don’t you fuss. It could honestly be that he forgot, the way that man is.”

Troy’s Uncle Henri Martel was his mother’s brother, and he *could* be a little scatterbrained at times. He owned a vineyard along the French Riviera —or he had, at least, before the war. It seemed to Troy that everything had changed since then, and he didn’t know what his mother’s beautiful France would look like after it was all over.

Of course, Troy had never been to France. His mother reminisced often, but she’d come to England with Papa just after their marriage and hadn’t left since. She’d always planned on returning when Troy and Lola were a bit older, but they’d not gotten to it, and then the war came.

Troy wasn’t a fan of the romantic, but he constantly heard his parents’ love story nonetheless. It was Papa’s favorite to tell—traveling to France in the late 1890s on a holiday, meeting a girl who stopped him in his tracks, marrying her scarcely half a year later, taking her to England, making a home with her.

“I’m sure he wouldn’t just forget, though,” said Maman, shaking her head. “*Mon chéri* Henri. He loves me very much.”

"But he is a bit of a scatterbrain, dear. You must remember that, although I know you're his favorite." Papa patted his wife's hand. He took a sip of his tea. "Doesn't hurt a thing that he's leaving Troy and Lola a nice little sum upon his death."

Maman swatted his arm. "Oh, *se comporter, chéri*. That's years away—or at least we hope so." Her lovely eyes darkened, and Troy glared at his father. Even Papa wasn't allowed to make *Maman* sad. No one was.

"I'm sorry, Estelle. That wasn't appropriate." Papa cocked his head. "But really. Don't worry, dear."

"I try not to." Maman sighed. "Anyway, we can't keep you away from work any longer, *chéri.* I'll see you at six?"

"Six. If I'm a minute over, dump my plate on the street and denounce me for a heretic." He stood and gave her a peck on the cheek. He ruffled Troy's hair, gave Lola another hug, and walked out the door.

"And you two should be on your way to school soon," Maman said, rising and making her way to the stove. "Straight there and then straight back. We've studying to do, and Lola needs to clean her side of the room."

Lola laughed. "I guess I do! It gets so terribly messy, and I don't know quite why. But that's all right."

"All right, *oui*. But it must be picked up this afternoon." Maman kissed her daughter and then Troy on both cheeks—she wouldn't stop kissing him regardless of his feelings on the subject, but he'd learn to accept that.

Then she handed Troy a lunch box and sent them out the door.

~

Maman glanced over Troy's shoulder. "I'm still not sure you've done that right, *chéri,* but we'll have to wait until your papa comes home to check." She winked and kissed the cowlick at his crown.

Troy slid the sheet of paper full of equations away and set the pencil on top of it. "What time is it?"

"6:30. But that's not so bad. He could be delayed." Maman ran a hand over her face and went to the window, peering out into the street. "It could be anything; I'm not worried."

"Are you going to dump his plate on the street?" Lola nodded towards the neatly set table. "That's what he said to do."

Maman laughed softly. "*Non*, I'm not going to dump his plate on the street, *chéri.* Nor am I going to denounce him a heretic. Sometimes you have to be a bit more patient with your husband—that's something you learn after you're married fifteen years."

"I guess so," said Lola doubtfully. She probably thought it'd be awfully funny. Troy thought it'd be rather funny, too, but he didn't particularly like that his father was so late.

"He'll be home any moment now, and he'll have an explanation, and that's all there is to it." Maman walked away from the window to the stove where she pulled a pan off. "I think he'd want us to eat, though—so let's begin."

Lola pulled back her seat, holding it with both arms, then climbed up, and Troy put away his school books and pushed her in so her chin was even with the table.

Troy set his jaw. "I think I'll wait for Papa and eat with him."

"*Non, chéri.*" Maman began serving plates. "Take a seat, and we'll all eat together. Your Papa will probably be home in five minutes, and he'll catch up to us. Close your eyes; would you like to say the *prière*, Troy?"

Troy nodded and folded his hands. "Dear God, thank you for this day. Please help Papa come home soon. Please let him not be hurt or lost or anything, and please let his day not have been too hard. Amen."

"Amen," echoed Maman and Lola.

Troy opened his eyes and met his mother's across the table. "He's got to come home now, right?"

"*Oui*. Soon, Troy, soon. Or I shall call the office if he doesn't. I don't want to bother him if he's halfway home or just having to stay late to take care of something."

"I suppose so," said Troy. He ate his potato stew with frequent glances at Lola. Even her consistent bubbliness had faded a bit, though she smiled cheerily whenever she met his eyes. She seemed toned down, the worry probably brought on by her mother and brother.

Troy winced. He didn't want his own fears to transfer over to Lola! That wouldn't make him a very good big brother, now, would it?

He grinned big and took an enormous bite of his roll. “He’ll be home any minute, though. I know it. After all, he wouldn’t want us to dump his plate on the street!”

Lola smiled, and Troy knew his job was accomplished.

“Don’t talk with your mouth full.” Maman rose from her seat impatiently and went to the window as the words passed her lips by rote.

“Sorry.”

Maman didn’t reply as she pulled back the white lace curtain and peeked out into the street below. “*Qu’est-ce qui le retient?*”

What keeps him? was indeed a valid question. Troy wished he had the answer.

Maman returned to her seat and finished eating her supper in silence.

The door flipped open, and a man stood in the doorway, hand on the edge of the frame. He leaned heavily against it, acting as if it were the only thing keeping him standing.

It took Troy a full minute to recognize his father’s face, so scarred by fresh cuts and bruises it was. He leaned heavily against it, acting as if it were the only thing keeping him standing.

“*Chéri!*” Maman ran to his side. “What happened?” She tentatively touched his face then placed a hand on his shoulder. “Can you stand? *Chéri,* let me help you.”

Troy watched blankly as his father put his arm around his mother’s shoulder and leaned on her to make it across the kitchen to a seat at the table.

"What happened? I was mad with worry. We all were." Maman wet a cloth and rubbed it gently over the dried blood that caked his father's face, especially about his cracked lip and slightly crooked nose.

Still, Papa winced and caught her hand. "Give me a moment, Estelle."

"I … I …" Her hands were shaking, and she set the cloth on the table. "Can you breathe?"

"Through my mouth." Papa drew a shaky breath in. It rattled oddly, and Troy stepped forward then back. He reached for Lola and pulled her close. Her eyes were very big, and Troy let her bury her face in his stomach for a moment, stroking the red-gold ringlets.

Papa sat there, arms braced against the table, panting.

"Can you tell me?" Maman whispered. "How did you walk home? What happened?"

"Not … not with the children here." He drew a deep shaky breathe. "They can't … can't hear this."

Maman glanced across the room and met Troy's eyes then her eyes flickered down to her trembling daughter. "Troy, Lola, go to the other room."

"But *Maman—*"

"*Aller. À présent.*"

Troy shuffled into the parlor, holding Lola's hand, and slid the door shut. As Lola walked across the room and sat in a chair, Troy put his ear to the door.

"Now, tell me," Maman was saying, "and then let me decide if we should call a doctor to set your nose."

"There's not much he could do for that, I'm afraid. Might have a bit of a crook in it after this." There was a pause, and Troy guessed his father was examining his facial features for further damage. "Got a rather nasty bump to the head, too, that put me out for—oh, what time is it?"

"About seven."

"Oh, I didn't realize. I was unconscious for more than half an hour then." A heavy sigh that turned into a low moan. "So yes, a doctor. But I want to tell you first."

"*Vite, vite, mon chéri.*"

A long pause, then Papa began. "I was just walking home from work, as always, when a group of young men—I'd say they were all fifteen, sixteen, seventeen years old—confronted me. There were about ten of them, I think. Asked me why I wasn't … wasn't in France. I told them I didn't believe in the war, that I thought it was pointless."

"Oh, *chéri.*" Maman's tone was reproachful. "You know very well you shouldn't have told them that!"

"I can't lie, dear."

"I know, but … you could have just walked past them. They were just boys; they wouldn't have bothered you if you simply brushed them off." A heavy sigh. "But you had to go on about your beliefs. Pacifism isn't popular, *chéri.* I'll support you in anything you decide, but only as long as you're not getting yourself killed."

"Well, I didn't get killed."

"*Près de là!*"

"No, not even near to it."

"So they *just* dragged you into an alley and beat you? Left you unconscious? Broke your nose, probably gave you a serious head injury?"

“It’s not serious, dear.”

“It looks serious!”

“Once we get some of this blood cleaned up, it won’t be so bad.” Papa sighed. “Call for a doctor now, if it will make you feel better.”

“It will.” Maman’s footsteps clicked across the room, and Troy scrambled back as the door opened. “Troy, can you run for a doctor? Murray will do.”

Troy nodded and hurried to do as his mother said, but a heavy weight had entered his chest.

He trusted his father. Respected him. But soldiers marching and war banners flying were exciting, and he wished his father could be a hero like the fathers of the other boys at his school.

He wished sometimes he didn’t hear whispers of “coward’s son,” among his schoolmates. He hated how his faithless heart wished his father would just join up and be a hero like everyone else’s.

But that just wasn’t his father. His father wasn’t someone who wanted to be a hero—he just wanted peace. Troy wanted peace, too, but he also wanted to help his country win this war. He believed in England —and in France, too.

Chapter Two

Papa was all right, as it turned out. His face had to be bandaged until it was almost all obscured, and his nose would never be perfectly straight again, but it appeared the bump on his head wasn't too terrible.

Afterwards, Papa and Maman stayed up long into the night talking about the next step for the family. Troy knew this because he couldn't resist tiptoeing to listen at the door after Lola was asleep that night.

"But I wouldn't have you give in to man's opinions," Maman said softly in French. They generally spoke in French late at night, thinking Troy and Lola couldn't understand it as well as English—but they both could. Growing up with a mother who rattled on in another language day and night generally led to one speaking that language fairly fluently.

"I know, Estelle." Papa sighed. "It's just … it's just that … I see the look in Troy's eyes. And I think I owe as much to him—and to Lola—as I do to personal convictions. It's through luck that my number hasn't come up in the draft, but we have decided that, should I be forced to join the army at any time, I would. But perhaps I should join—"

"And risk your life for something you don't believe in?"

There was a long silence, then Papa answered. "I wonder sometimes if I believe the right things. If my desire to be a peacemaker rather than a fighter isn't clouding my sense of what God really asks of a man, and of me in particular. So many men in the Bible were warriors …"

"But not all! And not you."

"Have I really considered the option, though? Have I really opened my heart to God's plans for my life?"

Another silence. "I can't answer that. I know I'm not God, to dictate what your life will be like. To dictate whether you join the army or not, die or not. Even to dictate what your feelings should be. I love you, and I want you to stay close to me."

"I know, dearest."

"But … I say if you feel that you've made the wrong choice, then I will continue to love you and support you and …" Her voice broke a bit. "If you die, I will attempt to bear it as I know it is His will which dictates who dies and who lives, and nothing can touch you without Him having planned it."

"But as far as the morals go, do you think …?"

"Jesus Christ was a peacemaker, darling. He is our first model. But He was also a warrior. That He would fight for a good cause and fight bravely. We've already talked about respecting the laws of your country so far as you can."

"Yes. But in this case, law doesn't really have a thing to do with it." Troy could hear the exhaustion in Papa's voice. "It has to do with whether or not I can take another beating like that."

A long silence. "We could move."

"And leave our home? The children's school? Our friends and neighbors? My work?"

"It wouldn't be a home without you, whatever we do."

He sighed. "I think I'd better just think about it for a bit."

"Pray, you mean."

"Exactly." Troy could hear the smile in his father's voice.

~

One evening two weeks later, Papa and Maman sat down with their son and daughter in the living room for a serious conversation.

"Your *Maman* and I have discussed this for some time, and we believe we've come to a sound conclusion." Papa glanced briefly at his wife. "We know this will take some getting used to, but I've decided to join the army."

Speechless, Troy glanced from Lola to his mother before flicking his eyes back to Papa. "What?"

"I'll probably be in France," Papa continued. "Odds of survival may in fact be quite low. These might be our last weeks together. But it's in God's hands."

His voice was so calm while Troy felt like he was falling apart. His heart beat hard, his stomach twisted in an odd way, and his throat choked, threatening to cut off his air supply.

He'd never quite understood why his father didn't want to join up—didn't know why it was a moral stand he needed to make. Perhaps, even, it was slightly cowardly, though Troy didn't believe his father could be a coward. He was Troy's hero—always had been.

It confused him—two separate and incongruent halves of the same man.

However, he'd wanted his father to stand up for his beliefs. To be the kind of man who could be counted on to stick with what he thought was right no matter what.

It made Troy wonder if there was anything his father would not renege on if pressured enough. If *beaten* enough, he supposed he ought to say.

Yet he couldn't let his father know about these thoughts.

"I … I suppose …" He struggled for the right words. Tact was never his strong suit. "It will be good to have a war hero for a father."

Papa glanced at his wife. "Has it been hard for you, Troy?"

He shook his head, then nodded slightly. "Not bad, Papa. But … there has been … well, Jimmy did say—" But he stopped himself, confused.

"What did Jimmy say?" Maman prompted.

"Well, it's not true," Troy clarified, "but he said Papa was a coward; that he was scared to join up and die like Jimmy's father." He flinched saying the words, but they weren't his own.

This brought a new layer of determination to

Papa's face. Troy was almost scared of the expression, and he was certainly curious about the look and nod exchanged between his mother and father.

Had he just sealed his father's fate? He hoped not. Wasn't their decision already made, after all? Or had they still been lingering before he told them about the bullying? He'd hate to have sent his father to war just because he was getting teased a bit. That was hardly anything, and nothing he couldn't handle. He was taller than every boy in his class, anyway.

"That's fine, Troy. As long as we're clear that it's not true. I suppose this will rather clear things up for Jimmy. Now let's talk about what will happen next."

Troy listened, heart beating hard, as Papa explained the day he was due to report for training, how long that would likely be, how he'd go to France after that.

How he loved them. How he'd write every chance he got, and he wanted them to write constantly to him, too. That he knew their letters would keep him going because his love for them would be the only reason to live.

Troy decided to spend the next weeks, months, years—however long it was until God brought Papa back to London—praying.

~

Before he left, Papa had a few days when he was done with his job as a clerk at a big bank and had time to spend with his family. After Troy came home, he'd work with him with mathematics for a bit then spend the rest of the evening with his family.

They played games or just chatted, but either way, the times were wonderful. The nearness of his father's leaving made Troy realize what a wonderful blessing they had in each other—and how central his dear Papa was to him.

He loved his father. He needed him for his advice and company and talking and the joy it brought to his *Maman*'s eyes to spend time with him and the way Lola cuddled into his broad chest.

On the last night, after dinner, Troy ran to fetch his mathematics book as always, but Papa stopped him.

"I'd like us to take a walk, son." Papa reached for their coats. "Put this on. There's a nip in the air."

Curious, Troy shrugged on his jacket and followed his father down the stairs from their rented home. Out on the streets, Papa reached for Troy's hand. Since it was the last night, he didn't mind.

"I have some things to tell you, Troy. I would have waited until you were a bit older, but now I worry … well, I might not get another opportunity."

"All right," said Troy. He didn't want to think that his father might not come back, but he did want to hear this advice.

"I don't know quite what to start with." Papa smiled softly. "I suppose I should start by saying that I know you are a decent boy. Your mother and I did our best to raise you to honor God in every way possible, and a good Christian makes a great man."

Troy nodded.

"Which is why I think, if you keep the faith, you have the ability to go far—further than most. I believe that you are more than capable of whatever you set your mind to … but I also believe that God has a plan for your life, and that through listening to Him you can find your most perfect future."

Papa took a deep breath. "And here we get to some things I would have rather told you at fifteen or sixteen, when you were already thinking on them, but I suppose it will have to be now. I suppose you know you must always respect women?"

"Yes." He didn't exactly understand why men made such a big bother about the female half of the race—other than his mother and Lola, he didn't care for them—but he did know that a real man didn't hurt them.

"There's a lot to know about women, Troy. A lot I can't tell you now, a lot that would require your mother to fill in should the need arise. But for now, I think you should know that being married to a good woman is, well, it can make a difference in your life in ways you can't even begin to imagine. And I'm not saying you have to get married. Some men stay single by choice, and there isn't a thing about that which is wrong or ungodly."

Troy was glad of that, because he didn't want to get married—ever.

"But if you do choose to get married—I should say if you are called to marriage—I don't want you to settle for anything less than a woman who will build you up and be your best friend, not tear you down. Your mother is my best friend; she has been since we married. She has always been a blessing to me. Our marriage wasn't always perfect." He smiled. "No one's perfect, and you can't go looking for the perfect woman. Just the one who brings out the best in you and is willing to seek God in your life together."

That all sounded quite wise, but it didn't really apply as Troy wasn't going to get married because girls were disgusting. Except his mother and sister, of course.

"And I can see I've lost your attention, so I'll stop." Papa smiled. "Don't worry about it too much. It'll all come in time."

Troy doubted that, but he just squeezed his father's hand and kept walking on with him.

"I don't know what else I could tell you," Papa said after a long silence. "I don't know what else is important other than God. Stay close to your mother, of course, and your sister. Protect them always. You'll be the man of the house while I'm gone."

"I'll make sure nothing happens to them."

"That's good. A man should always care for the women in his life." Papa sighed then smiled. "Let's go back to the house now, son."

Chapter Three

Months passed. Spring melted into summer which melted into autumn, and then Christmas came. The war dragged on and on. Troy doubted it would ever stop.

Papa wrote when he could and Troy scribbled at least a few words to him every day in return. There were also special sealed letters that only Maman read —and which, Troy's jealous mind thought, were thicker and more frequent. But he supposed he oughtn't to mind, really, and they did make *Maman* smile so.

They also brought a shadow to her blue eyes that he didn't particularly care for, but that was to be expected. It was a bit sad to hear from someone who one loved very much but couldn't be near.

Christmas 1917 was difficult for the Kees. Money ran short, but that wasn't much of an issue. They were used to it. It was Papa not being there that was the problem—it was not being a complete family.

Troy tried to step in as man of the house as his

father suggested, but he wasn't sure quite how to do that. Lola didn't really care to listen to him—which made sense, as he was her brother, not her father, and had no real business bossing her around—and Maman seemed to find any attempts at manhood adorable rather than taking them with the seriousness they deserved.

But Christmas passed, and 1918 came. As far as Troy could tell, things didn't seem to be getting better. All around him people were losing loved ones to this terrible war, and he began to hear rumors that all of the world was falling sick with a terrible case of influenza that left hospitals reeling and families even less complete than before.

And still the war went on and on and on. And still the influenza caused half of his schoolmates' families to go into mourning.

When he and Lola arrived home from school that day, they were surprised to see the windows blacked out. They jogged up the stairs—the door was unlocked, and they slipped in. No lights were on; the whole place was still. Troy sniffed and glanced about the kitchen. No hint of supper. What could be wrong?

"Where's *Maman*?" Lola asked in a very small voice.

Troy glanced down. Her blue eyes were brimming with tears. He forced a grin on his face. "Well, I'm sure she hasn't fallen down the rabbit hole!" He advanced into the house. "*Maman! Maman*, where are you?"

There was a long silence before he heard his mother's voice from her bedroom, soft and weak. "In here, *chéri*. Come … bring Eloise."

Lola and Troy walked together to their parents' bedroom. Maman sat on the edge of her bed, eyes red-rimmed, but she forced a smile.

"Come sit with me." She reached her arms out to them.

Lola ran across the room and jumped on her mother's lap, throwing her arms about her neck. "Is everything all right, *Maman*?"

Maman took a deep but shaky breath. "*Oui*. We're all right. We're … we're together, so we're going to be all right." She buried her face in Lola's curls. "Come here, Troy. You, too."

Troy dragged his feet across the room and took a seat at his mother's side.

"*Je suis désolé*. I've probably scared you." Maman wrapped her arm around his son. "It's all right. Really. I have you two. What … what more could I want?" She snuggled Troy into her side. "*Mes bébés*, I received a message from the war office today."

"Can Papa come home?" Lola jumped up and grinned. "Soon? When?"

Troy stared at his mother in disbelief. "Is he dead?"

Maman reached for her daughter to draw her close. "Killed in action over a week ago. He's gone, *chéri*."

Troy blinked and blinked again. He swallowed, ran a hand over his eyes, stared at the wall.

His mother said soft comforting words about Heaven through the crack in her voice, fighting the tears, perhaps even fighting the realization. Troy heard her vaguely, wrapped his arm around her waist, kept her and Lola both close to him.

"But don't you worry, *mes bébés*. I'm going to take care of you both." Maman closed her eyes for a moment. "Your *oncle* Henri will probably come for us after the war is over."

"We'll live in France?" Troy whispered.

"*Oui*. Probably. I don't know for sure. But wherever we are, England or France or … or Germany—"

"Why would we go to Germany?" Lola asked, eyes wide.

"Well, *chéri*, what I mean is, no matter where we go, God will be with us." Maman ran her fingers through her daughter's hair. "We'll get through this. We'll be all right. Don't worry."

"I … I can't believe it." Troy's chest heaved, and his vision seemed to fade around the edges, a sort of vicious blackness superseding over his eyes, his mind. "Could there be a mistake? Could … he can't really be gone. He can't! He said he'd come back! He said—" His voice was hysterical now, and a large lump in his throat hindered his breathing.

"Shush, Troy. Shush." His mother kissed the top of his head. "I know. I know, I felt the same. I've … I've been fighting it all this afternoon. But I'm sure."

"How can we be sure?" Troy stood. "Maybe it was a mistake!"

"*Non, chéri.* I'm so sorry. So sorry for all of us. I … I'll miss him more than you know, and I … I can't wait to see him in Heaven some day. I …" A tear slid down her cheek. "I don't know what I'm going to do without him. He's … he's so much a part of me! But that doesn't mean we—all of us—can't go on. We must."

Troy couldn't believe it. He couldn't believe that his father had died in a war he didn't believe in. Couldn't believe that he wouldn't see Papa again. Wouldn't watch him smile, hear his voice, laugh at his dark sense of humor, be tutored in math and teased over his ineptitude in the subject.

He couldn't believe that … that God had let this happen.

"Does God still love us?" His voice was hushed, but his mother caught it.

"*Oui*. He always loves us." Maman squeezed her son's shoulders. "But sometimes it's all right to question. God is prepared for all our questions. You can go to Him."

Troy nodded stiffly. He knew that, but it was so odd to have to realize it in a moment of crisis. That there would be times when he didn't actually feel like God loved him at all—when he doubted and hated.

"I'm sorry," he said, as much to God as his mother.

"Don't be sorry." She kissed his cheek. "*Tout est bien*. I know."

~

The war was over in France. Bells rang, people cheered, the world came alight. But for Troy, and in the Kee home, the war wasn't quite over.

It had left a mark that would not soon be erased from hearts, from souls. Troy doubted he could ever smile again.

It had been six months, and still his mother cried

herself to sleep. She put on an act during the day, all smiles, and wept softly into the nights.

Troy and Lola would creep into her room and snuggle into her, and eventually she gave up all pretenses and let them sleep there with her. Troy would have preferred his own bed on a regular basis, but if his mother was crying, he wanted to be there. After all, wasn't he truly the man of the house now?

Troy tried his best to sort out the issues with God, but it was hard. Everything had been ripped out from under him. He didn't understand. If God loved him, why take away his father?

He and Lola had dropped out of school months ago, when they received the telegram. He supposed now that the war was over, they'd be going back, but Troy didn't want to. Besides, he might have to see if he couldn't get some sort of job.

They were without support, and money was running low. There was nowhere to turn in England, but now that the war was over, at least they might get in contact with Henri Martel, Maman's brother.

There had been no word for months, though, and *Maman* worried that he, too, had been killed. But there had been no notice, so she continued to remain optimistic.

"So for the time being at least, we can count on *oncle* Henri. Later, we'll worry about it should he be dead."

Troy sighed, feeling older than twelve. "If he's alive, why doesn't he come find us? Why doesn't he answer your letters?"

Maman simply shook her head. "*Dieu seul sait.*"

~

In the past, Maman would be up before the children, dancing about the kitchen, singing, waking them with kisses and hugs, cooking breakfast and seeing that they were well-fed before she sent them off to school.

The Kee children still hadn't returned to school after the death of their father, and Maman still wasn't singing or dancing, but she did get up early to cook them a nutritious breakfast every day.

Today, she did this as usual, but halfway through breakfast Troy noticed that her face was flushed, and she repeatedly placed her hand to her forehead or her stomach. Her coffee was untouched.

"Are you all right, *Maman*?"

She attempted a smile, but it turned into a wince. "I don't know. I think I'll lie down and get some extra rest."

Troy's brow wrinkled. "All right. Call if you need us."

"I will," Maman assured him. "*J'taime*, Troy. *J'taime*, Eloise."

Toward the afternoon, Troy made sandwiches for him and Lola then took another to the closed door of his mother's bedroom. He paused there for a second before rapping softly.

No response.

He put his ear to the door and listened.

He could *hear* his mother breathing. Now, it wasn't that the walls were particularly thick or the door particularly tight, but regardless of the walls, one shouldn't be able to hear their mother breathing from outside the door.

Her breaths were ragged and uneven, ending in a soft moan at the end as if it pained her to breathe. He opened the door and stepped in.

"Troy, stop there! Don't come a step closer." His mother pushed herself up off the pillow. She was shivering to the point of convulsions, but her voice was firm. "I mean it. Back out and close the door."

"But *Maman*—!"

"Obey."

Troy took a step back. "Shall I call the doctor?"

"Let me tell you what to do first." She paused and pressed a hand to her head then fell back against the pillow.

"*Maman*?"

"Don't … don't come into this room, Troy. I think … *non*, I know. I have the Influenza, Troy. I need you to tell Lola to go to your room and stay there. She can't … she can't come in, either. Make her obey."

"I will," Troy said. "But … shall I run for a doctor?"

"If the worst happens, I need you to contact your *oncle* Henri. He has money, a house, and he will do his best by you. It's not what I wanted, but …" Her voice trailed off, and she pulled the covers close about her, still trembling all over.

"The doctor, though, *Maman*? The doctor?"

"I … *oui*. The doctor." She nodded jerkily. "Only make sure Lola doesn't come near. I don't know if she'll listen to me—she'll want to play nurse, and I can't let her. Not when … when it spreads so easily. I've read about it."

Troy nodded. He had to. The disease infected fast. Fine and well in the morning, dead by evening. But that wouldn't be *Maman*, surely. She'd be one of the people who got over it in a few days.

Lola came up behind him. "What's wrong with *Maman*?"

Troy looked down at her and made himself smile. "A bit offish. I'm going for a doctor. You go to your room and stay there."

"Oh, I shall be her nurse!" said Lola gleefully.

"*No*," Troy said sharply. He closed the door to his mother's room. "You will go to our room and stay there. Understand me?"

Lola scowled but marched to the other bedroom.

Troy ran out of the door. Their regular doctor wasn't at his house, so he was obliged to run to a nearby hospital—and then wait. It was a full two hours until he returned with an exhausted elderly man. They hurried up the stairs to the Kee's apartment, and Troy led the doctor straight to his Maman's bedroom. The door was open, and Lola stood just inside, eyes wide.

"Lola! I told you not to leave your room!" Troy ran past her. His mother was unconscious now, but continued to toss and turn against the bed, moaning and thrashing. The room smelled of sickness.

Troy shuddered at the sight, but he'd brought the doctor. Surely he could make her better. Surely there was some medicine, some antidote.

"She's bad, son," the doctor said softly. "It's in a late stage."

How could he even know? He'd barely looked at her. "But she will get better?"

The doctor's face was grave. "Perhaps, but …" He sighed and stepped to the bedside, set his bag on the edge, and opened it.

A gasping sound issued from Maman's mouth followed by a series of convulsions. The doctor reached for her shoulders and pressed her down into the bed. At last Maman held still and seemed to breathe a bit, though her pants were haggard. A gurgling came with every breath.

"What … what's wrong with her?" Troy asked.

"Their chests get filled with fluid," the doctor mumbled. "She's drowning in it."

Lola gasped softly. "But can't you … can't you help her?"

The doctor stepped away from the bed. "I don't think so, dear." He glanced at Troy. "Why don't you take your sister out of here? This isn't something for a little girl to see."

Troy took Lola by the shoulders and forced her to leave the room ahead of him. "Shall … shall I come back?"

The doctor sighed. "No. Don't come back, son. Not until I call you."

Troy closed the door behind him and Lola, and they waited in the kitchen. It was less than half an hour later that the doctor emerged.

"I'm sorry. She's passed on." The doctor glanced between the two children. "It was too late for her."

"But … but she was fine this morning," Lola gasped out.

"I know. That's often how it is. This thing is the Black Death of the 20th century." The doctor growled low in his throat. "Where is your father?"

"D-dead," Troy stuttered out. "Dead in France."

"Have you any relatives?"

Troy shook his head. "Except our *oncle* Henri. He's in France."

"Friends? Someone to stay with?"

"No."

The doctor sighed and shifted his bag in his arms. "Come with me, then."

"But *Maman*!"

"She doesn't need you now, but you have to stay somewhere for the night. My wife and I can find a place to put two more children, I'm sure."

~

Dr. Hostetler had half a dozen other children bedded down on the floor of the parlor in his small house.

"Best we can do, but at least it's warm and clean and there'll be breakfast in the morning," he said as he laid out a blanket for Troy and Lola.

"Thank you," said Troy. He'd been replying with little polite things like that recently. He felt blessedly numb. Lola had been sobbing since *Maman* died, but not Troy. It was like his heart and soul hadn't caught up with his brain that told him his mother was gone forever.

"You're quite welcome, son," said the doctor.

Mrs. Hostetler came in then and cooed and fussed over Lola; washed her face, combed her hair, cuddled her close. She would have done the same with Troy if he'd let her, but he combed his own hair and washed his own face, and then after Mrs. Hostetler left, he cuddled Lola all night, which was enough for him.

Would he ever be able to cry again? He wasn't sure.

Chapter Four

The next day, Dr. Hostetler "took care of things" as concerned Maman's body. Their little house's lease was up in a few weeks, anyway, which, Dr. Hostetler said, was fortunate.

There wasn't much in the apartment worth keeping. Clothing, a few personal items, sheets and blankets and pillows. Dr. Hostetler let Troy and Lola pile them in the corner of his parlor.

The table, beds, and various kitchen pieces they sold or left. Wherever they went, Dr. Hostetler said, they probably wouldn't need furniture.

They tried to get a message off to *oncle* Henri, but chances were he wouldn't come. They'd still not heard a bit about him. He was probably dead. And there was no one else.

It truly felt that they were abandoned. No one to help them. Even God didn't seem to be helping. Who was there to turn to? They couldn't live in the Hostetler's parlor forever.

The weeks slid by. Children came and went, but

Troy and Lola stayed on. The Hostetlers were kind, and Troy was glad they had somewhere to stay that was safe and didn't require him to know too much about the next step in their life, but he was also eager to get on with things. To move forward.

He couldn't remain lost in the grief of his mother and father's passing forever. He wanted things to be settled. He wanted to discover what family would be like without them. There was him and Lola, and he'd always be her brother and she his baby sister, but—would *oncle* Henri be a part of their life? Or would they go to an orphanage? Would they never have a real family again?

Lola was trying to keep positive, and in many ways she succeeded better than Troy ever would. However, he was afraid she didn't fully grasp what had happened. She certainly didn't realize what danger they were in, alone in London with no one to help them.

Then one morning a knock on the door was heard. Troy, who was reading a story to Lola in the parlor, rose and went to answer it.

A tall man who looked to be younger than a father but older than a college boy stood there. He wore a big frown and a messy suit, and his hat was half-pulled over his gray eyes. He was almost painfully skinny and angular.

"Hello," said Troy.

"Hello." The man's accent had a slight twist that took Troy a moment to identify—but he soon realized it was French. "Who are you?"

"Troy Kee." Troy puffed up his chest. "Who are you?"

"Millard Harrington."

Troy blinked. What kind of name was that?

"That's silly!" Lola giggled.

Troy whirled to his sister. "Shush!"

"That's all right. It is a stupid name." Mr. Harrington brushed past Troy and Lola into the house. "What is this place?"

"It's Dr. and Mrs. Hostetler's home," Troy said with dignity. "Do you know them?"

"Er, no. Not really. Do you?"

"Not for long. The doctor came to see our *Maman* when she died, and he took us home with him." Troy fought back the burning behind his eyes, as he'd been doing for weeks.

"Hmm. What was your *Maman*'s name?"

"Estelle Kee."

"*Son nom de jeune fille.*"

It took Troy a moment to catch the language—he'd spoken nothing but English for the last three weeks.

But, thankfully, Mr. Harrington's pronunciation was perfect, or Troy wouldn't have been able to pick it up at all. This Millard fellow was asking for *Maman*'s maiden name.

"Martel," Troy said at last.

"Hmm," said Mr. Harrington again. He reached into the breast pocket of his coat and pulled out a scrap of paper. He unfolded it and passed it to Troy. "Is this her?"

Troy took the photograph and scanned it. It was his mother's face, all right, only younger. "*Oui*."

A ghost of a smile flickered about the man's eyes, but his lips didn't even move. "Good."

"Where did you get this?" Troy asked.

"From your *oncle* Henri."

"Is *oncle* Henri coming for us soon?" Lola piped up.

"*Non.*" Harrington cocked his head. "He was dead on a French battlefield a year ago. But he told me to come find his sister and make sure everything transferred over to her. However, when I arrived at the vineyard, lo and behold, here's a message informing me of the death of Madame Kee and the existence of two orphans." A sort of snorting laugh escaped. "Well, I hadn't much of a choice but to come."

"*Oncle* Henri's dead?" Lola asked in a very small voice.

"Yes, he is."

"But who are you?" Troy was just a bit suspicious of this random man who seemed to know so much about his family.

"A friend of his," said Harrington. "I used to live at his vineyard on and off. I'm a bit of an eccentric—I'm English, but I've lived in France these last nine years since I turned eighteen. I've no family, and I like it there. So I traveled around, did a bit of this and that, learned a lot, met your uncle, and helped him manage his vineyard. Joined the French army with him when it came to that."

That seemed straightforward enough to Troy. He supposed he'd like to do something like that—wander around and learn things and meet new people. It sounded like the perfect life. Though he couldn't, of course, as his responsibility was to Lola, and she probably wouldn't like that sort of life.

"So what are you here for?" Troy asked.

"To bring you to the vineyard. It's yours, or it will be. I'm Henri's caretaker for the time being. I'm sure we can get the legalities sorted so you can come into full possession when you're grown."

"But we can't live at a vineyard alone!" Troy protested. "I'm only twelve. That's not old enough to take care of Lola."

"Well, I'd be there, or so I'd presume."

Mrs. Hostetler entered the room just then. "Why, whatever is going on?"

"This man is Mr. Harrington!" said Lola. "He's the caretaker of our *oncle* Henri's things. And he's come for us."

Mrs. Hostetler was even more suspicious than Troy, and she insisted Harrington sit down and tell her all about it. As it turned out, Millard Harrington was telling the truth. He was even able to produce official documentation for much of what he said.

"So we'll go with him?" Lola asked.

"Yes," said Mrs. Hostetler.

"Good. We're leaving for France in two weeks. I imagine there are a few loose ends to tie up here." Harrington glanced between Troy and Lola. "So it's Troy and Eloise? Hmm."

"She goes by Lola," said Troy.

Harrington smirked. "Well, that's almost as stupid as Millard."

"It is not!" Lola stuck out her bottom lip and crossed her arms defensively.

"It is, too," Harrington said. He put his hat back on and walked to the door. "Shall I come back for you tomorrow morning so we can start figuring things out?"

"All right," said Troy.

It would seem this new adventure they were embarking on with Mr. Millard Harrington would be one of the craziest yet. But, somehow, Troy felt a kind of peace about it.

Harrington might be grumpy, plain-spoken, and obviously done with the world, but he would take care of his charges. Troy was sure of it.

~

Troy thought things were bad in England, but it was worse in France. The countryside was war-torn. He hadn't known the meaning of that tossed-about phrase before. It meant annihilation. It meant nothingness. It meant that the entire country of France was dead.

He imagined it would look better in the spring when it wasn't so gray, if some of the vegetation returned.

Lola perched on Harrington's lap throughout the entire train ride despite the fact that he repeatedly stated that he didn't want her to sit on his lap.

Troy offered his lap, but Lola wanted the window seat while he preferred to sit on the inside of the compartment. Countryside rushing by made him dizzy.

At last they arrived in a tiny town in the south of France.

It was right next to the Mediterranean, and Troy couldn't stop staring out at the waters. It was beautiful—and he needed a bit of beauty just then.

Lola liked it a lot. She squealed over exotic shops and sand and all that nonsense. She was always enthusiastic like that.

However, she wasn't enthusiastic about her uncle's house. And neither was Troy.

Situated in the middle of the vineyard, the little house was tall and skinny, oddly built.

"Henri Martel," Harrington said, "was the only Frenchman in the history of the world who didn't care a bit about appearances—clothing, scenery, architecture. He built that house in the English style, and he encouraged his sister to marry an Englishman. He was made for another country, though he couldn't stand the cold, so I don't know how well it would have gone for him."

Troy laughed. He thought the idea of a Frenchman shivering away in London to be very funny—and it reminded him of his mother in a good way.

Harrington gave him an odd look. No wonder—Troy hadn't so much as smiled since he met him. Troy was surprised, too. What had possessed him?

The house had a wide front door and a veranda that hung off to the side. The roof was crumbling off, and there was barely any paint left.

The inside was worse; only half-furnished, dusty, cobwebby, and covered with sheets.

Harrington glanced around and shrugged. "It's, er, going to take some work."

Troy shrugged. Pessimistic Harrington had just made the most optimistic statement of the year.

"Well, we can work at it, can't we?" Troy asked at last. "Clean it up and fix it and make it into a home?"

Harrington almost smiled then. "Best let's get to work, then."

Between Troy, Lola, and Harrington, they managed to make a list of all the repairs they'd need to do. It wasn't going to be easy; it would be a long, hard project. However, neither was it impossible.

Someday the house in France would be a home. Someday the vineyard would truly be theirs.

Part III: Le Début

"So we beat on, boats against the current,
borne back ceaselessly into the past."

The Great Gatsby by F. Scott Fitzgerald

Chapter One

Spring 1927
Kent, England

Adele took a deep breath and let it out slowly. In her chest, fury bubbled like a pot of burning soup, but she kept her sullen expression in place. She was in the right. Anger would lead to tears which could be taken as regret. But she regretted nothing.

She was an adult now. An adult made decisions for herself away from her mother, and an adult shouldn't be punished for those decisions. Regardless of how many times she'd been told not to make them.

"Do you understand me?" Mother asked.

"I don't know," she mumbled.

"Adele Elizabeth!"

"I don't care if it's ladylike or not!" Adele stomped her foot. It was childish, but she needed to get this point across. "I wish you'd leave me be."

Mother closed her eyes briefly. When they opened, her gaze was hard as nails. "Adele, you are my daughter, and you are only eighteen years old. You still live in my house; your food and clothes are provided by me. You may not believe that I have any authority over you, but I do, and this time you have gone too far."

Adele ran her hand through her closely cropped brown hair, now just reaching past her chin, edges jagged. The rest of it lay on a heap in the bathroom sink. With all that extra weight gone, it was starting to curl. Adele smiled in spite of her mother's angry words. She felt more beautiful than she ever had before in her life.

She tossed her head. "I wanted to look fashionable for once. I'd like to get it styled. It's Millie's birthday party tomorrow, and all our friends will be there."

"Party? You're not going to a party anytime soon, young lady."

Adele gasped. "But I need to go to this party! Millie's going to be eighteen, and she needs my support! She doesn't have a lot of friends other than me, and she's shy around the ones she does have."

"That's too bad, because you can't go. This is absolutely reprehensible, Adele. Your hair was one of your best qualities. Besides, now it looks terrible."

Adele turned to the mirror and examined herself. What she saw was a rather pretty young lady with dark eyes and hair—vibrant, fashionable, daring. Yes, her hair was rough, but it could easily be styled. She also saw the curve of her hips which she disliked greatly, but once her mother stopped forcing fattening foods down her throat, she'd lose that extra "baby fat," as she called it, in a trice.

"It just needs to be trimmed," Adele said. "We'll go to the village today and—"

"Adele, no. I don't want anyone to see you like that."

"But—"

"No buts about it, young lady. I'm very disappointed in you."

Adele stomped into her room. That was nothing new. Her mother was *always* disappointed in her. It was unavoidable.

She briefly considered throwing herself on her bed and sobbing, but decided against it. She simply stood in the middle of the floor, breathing heavily, and thought.

It wasn't so much that she wanted to upset her mother. It was that she wanted to have her own way in the world, and this time cutting her hair was her own way. Adele considered her mother's way to be dowdy. Old-fashioned. Overly moralistic.

Always angry with her. Always disappointed in her. Always pummeling her with harsh words, insults, pure hatred.

"I'm eighteen. I'm old enough to make my own decisions. She can't control me anymore now that I'm an adult," Adele muttered to herself. "She's awful. She's cruel. She doesn't *understand* me."

Mother never understood her rebellious demon of a daughter. Didn't care whether she lived or died. She only wanted to make sure that Adele was firmly under her thumb with no hope of moving, no hope of breathing, no hope of being herself.

She closed her eyes and sighed. Her mother was just so … so *exacting*. Everything had to be her way.

Couldn't she see that Adele was her own person, that she must create her own life, have her own talents, face the world her way? But Mother didn't care about individuality. She only cared about being *ladylike*.

I'll leave. I'll go somewhere far away where she can't control me anymore. Millie and I will go together. I'll finally be free. I'll eat whatever I want —or nothing, if I choose to. I'll dress however I want, I'll go wherever I want with whomever I want, and no one and nothing will stop me. No one will even try.

This was a very satisfactory mental image, and Adele smiled. Trudging over to her bed, she sat down on the edge of it. *If Papa was here, none of this would have happened,* she reflected. *He would have let me style my hair however I wanted to. He would have let me have a boyfriend, too.*

In her heart, she knew this wasn't true—Papa had been just as strict as Mother. But she wanted to believe that her mother was the only cruel person in the world—or at least the most cruel.

Of course, it would be wondrous to have Kenneth there. Kenneth, Adele thought, was somewhat of a free spirit. Or at least that was how she remembered him. A wonderful intelligent, free man who did whatever he wanted with no regard for rules, authority, or Mother.

Adele wanted to be just like him … and she would grieve him until the day she died. Keep his memory alive in her heart by being like him—being free. Doing what she wanted. Living an adventurous, exciting, modern, glamorous life.

"Someday," Adele repeated, dropping her head on the pillow, "I'll get out of here. Someday, someday."

~

"There! That's as straight as I can make it!" Millie set the scissors on her vanity and stepped back. "I think it's cute. Or even, at least."

Adele glanced in the mirror. Thankfully, Millie had been able to help her in a way her mother never would. Though she still wasn't allowed to attend Millie's birthday party, Mother had sent her down to apologize for her upcoming absence. "Yes, that's nice. Thank you, Millie. I appreciate it." She rose and gave her best friend a hug.

"Well, I couldn't let you go around town looking like something the cat dragged in." Millie picked up a broom and began sweeping up the hair trimmings that had fallen on the hardwood floor of her bedroom. "But, Adele, you know—"

"You don't approve. I know, I know. Give me some grace, Millie. That old haircut was horrendous and went out of style when I was still a little girl! It's ridiculous."

Millie sighed. "I know it was difficult for you, especially since you appreciate style so. But respecting your mother—"

"Comes first. Trust me, Millie, I know it all. And I respect it! You be Millie and love on your parents and obey them even though you shouldn't have to anymore." Adele fluffed at her hair. "I'll be Adele and rebel against my horror of a mother who hates my soul."

"Oh, Adele, that's not—"

"True," Adele inserted.

Millie laughed. "It's funny the first few times, but if you don't stop finishing my sentences, I'm going to go insane. As I was saying, your mother—"

"Loves you. She must because she's my mother." Adele arched her eyebrows.

Millie glared at her.

"Oh, all right. I'll stop." She patted her hair one last time then went to the window. From Millie's bedroom, she could see the top of her roof up the road aways. She wondered what her mother was doing. Probably still pouting over her hair.

"It's just that I hate to see a mother and a daughter so quarrelsome when you're all the other has." Millie sighed. She often sighed when talking to Adele. Though Adele loved Millie—and vice-versa—they didn't agree on a great many points. Most points, actually.

"But your mother loves you, Millie. She also respects you and wants you to succeed …" Adele's voice trailed off. "You know what it's like with my mother. It's impossible to live with her. In fact—" She took a deep breath. "Millie, I think I'm going to leave home soon."

Millie gasped. "Adele! But where could you go?"

"To London, I think. That's where all the fun's to be had, and I know I'd love it there. I've always loved cities."

"But … but …" Millie blinked rapidly then thought of what she wanted to say next. "But you realize there'd be more to it than running away and having a grand old time! You'd need somewhere to sleep that's safe, food, clothing … all sorts of things. A job, first and foremost. And enough money to keep you going until your paycheck comes in."

"I have plenty put by," Adele said. At least, she had several months' worth of pocket money and bits and pieces she'd saved up by helping Millie's mother with gardening. Mrs. Lark was far more generous than she ought to be. "Enough to keep me for a few weeks, anyway."

"But where would you work?"

Adele shrugged. "I'd find something."

Millie stared at Adele for a moment then laughed nervously. "Surely you're joking, Adele? You can't be serious if you're this unprepared. You'll need to have a plan. Besides—I don't know that it's a good idea for you to leave home."

Adele huffed. "Well, what else could I do, Millie? I'm done with school; I don't want further education, and there's nothing I could do that would be useful. There aren't any opportunities for a girl like me in this town. My mother wants me to get married—but I don't want to! Married to one man, watching his children, cleaning his house? I'd go mad, Millie. You know I would."

Millie sighed. "Well, some don't get married, and there's not a thing wrong with that. But—"

"But I should be content with what I have? But I shouldn't want more than my simple lot? But I shouldn't reach for my dreams?"

Millie struggled with this. "Not … not exactly. It's just that … you see, Adele, there's a difference between goals and dreams. And I want you to have dreams and to reach for them. But I also want you to set goals, realistic goals, for reaching those dreams. It's because I love you very much, and I'd hate to see you become a prodigal son of sorts."

Adele wasn't very familiar with the Bible anymore, but she knew that story. Millie essentially meant she'd crash and burn in a few weeks and come crawling back to her mother, filthy and begging for mercy. "That won't happen to me. I'm going to make a success of this. You'll see. This is a different world than the one my mother grew up in. It's been vastly different since the war ended—but she can't, or won't, accept that fact."

"She's your mother, though. Regardless, you owe her respect."

Adele simply shook her head. "She's treated me too badly, Millie. You know the things she says to me. Dreadful things. I just need to be free of her for my own sanity. Please—please support me in this! I mean, you're going to London! How is that different?"

"I have a job lined up, and my parents approve. Papa helped me find the job!"

This was true. Millie had trained in various secretarial skills over the past year.

Unlike Mother, the Larks were raising a girl who would succeed in this world. Adele was very proud of Millie—she hoped she'd have a brilliant career in, well, secretarying. Or something bigger, should something bigger come along, which she assumed it would. Millie had that kind of luck.

"Could I come with you?" Adele said softly. Before Millie could speak, she rushed on. "We could share the apartment, which means you'd only have to pay half the rent, which means you'd be able to save up a whole lot more. I know you want to so you can buy some furniture if you get married or whatever you said."

Millie blushed. "That was my plan, yes. But—"

"I know you don't approve of me leaving without my mother's blessing. But I'm eighteen! And you know this will make your parents feel better. It's a scary world for you to be in alone."

"I have friends in London."

"But they won't live with you! They won't be there for you, night and day, whenever you need them." Adele gazed at Millie imploringly. "Please. You're my best friend, and you can help me get out of this horrid life I'm living. *Please*, Millie."

In the end, Millie couldn't resist Adele's pleading eyes. She nodded.

"Yes, I suppose you may. But remember, you've got to get a job first thing. In fact, we'll start looking for one and preparing for interviews before we go next month." Millie hesitated. "And of course this all hinges on my parents' agreement! You can't come with me unless they say it's all right."

Grinning, Adele gave Millie a hug that she was sure almost smothered her. "Thank you, thank you, thank you, Millie!"

Finally she'd be free.

~

The small apartment didn't allow for many possessions. Millie and Adele stayed in the same room with twin beds and kept their clothes in one chest of drawers.

It was nice, though. Very cozy.

In the first week, Adele managed to snag a job as an assistant at a department store. It was mostly fetching and carrying boxes, helping the saleswoman, and even a bit of polishing counters and organizing clothing, but it was work at a fashionable clothing sales place. The only thing that could make it better was working with flowers, but that wasn't a possibility.

Really, she'd like to own her own business some day, but that seemed a distant dream. For now, this was enough.

Within a month, Adele was chatting with customers and talking them into buying things, and a promotion to saleswoman followed not long after. She boasted that she could sell anyone anything—and it seemed rather true.

Adele could be charming when she wanted to be, and she was naturally chatty and people-oriented. She also knew how to describe something, how to make it seem necessary, how to convince people they must have this item.

Pride swelled in Adele's chest with every sale. Every article of clothing, every pair of shoes sold was another victory against her mother, against her past. Adele Collier would not be stopped.

Chapter Two

February 28th, 1928
French Riviera

"For he's a jolly good fellow, for he's a jolly good fellow," Lola sang as she set a plate in front of Troy containing a slice of pie which was obscured by candles. "And so say all of us!"

"Speak for yourself," said Harrington.

Troy chuckled. "My goodness, Lola! Why aren't the candles lit?"

"I couldn't light twenty-one candles without burning the house down, Troy, and you know it," Lola said. "Now eat your pie! It's your favorite. Apple."

"I can't eat my pie! There are a billion candles covering it!"

Lola laughed, her eyes twinkling. "There are not! There are twenty-one for my big brother's twenty-first birthday. Just pick them off!"

“I’ll die of starvation by the time I pick them off.” Troy wrapped his arm around Lola’s waist and gave her a side-hug. “Thank you. It’s perfect.”

Lola took a seat across from him and served a slice of apple pie to both herself and Harrington.

“What about birthday presents?” Troy asked around his first bite.

“Don’t talk with your mouth full.” Lola grinned. “Not much in the budget for birthday presents, of course, but we have a few. I think one’s21st birthday should be important!”

They ate in silence for a moment, then Lola piped up again.

“How are things going with financials? I know we’re tight.”

“Oh! Don’t you worry about that, dear.” Troy had made the mistake of letting it slip last month to Lola that things weren’t going well with the vineyard as far as money went, and he’d regretted it ever since. Not only was she pinching pennies—or rather francs—but she was almost worried.

Lola wasn’t meant to be worried.

He’d determined to keep it a secret from now on, no matter the cost.

“So it’s better?” Lola’s infectious smile appeared on her face, and Troy couldn’t help but feel it spread to him.

“It’s all better, dear.” He squeezed his hand and returned to his pie.

“So now that we’re back on track, will you shave off that peach fuzz?”

He’d teasingly told Lola a few weeks ago that he was attempting to grow a mustache because he couldn't afford razors. It had lightened the mood and been well worth humiliating his poor facial hair.

Troy ran his fingers over his upper lip. "I think it's grown out as it should."

Lola laughed. "Has not."

"Has, too!"

"Children, children," Harrington mumbled.

"It does make me look distinguished, doesn't it?" Troy demanded of Harrington.

"Eh," said Harrington. "He's right that it doesn't look awful … though what would convince a man not to shave is beyond me."

Troy chuckled. He was used to their jokes and teasing. He, for one, liked his mustache and intended to keep it. Only God could convince him to shave it off, and that seemed a silly request for God to make of him.

~

Lola danced along the street beside him. "I can't believe we're back in England! It's been so long."

Troy smiled down at her. He hadn't told Lola that they were going to England seeking a loan, that the vineyard needed it to stay open—only that he had business, and he wanted her to tag along to keep him company. She was growing into a lovely young woman—and she'd always been his dearest friend. Though perhaps it was a bit sad that his only true friend was his little sister.

He opened the door to one of the bank offices and walked up to a clerk sitting at the front.

"Hello. I'm Troy Kee, here to see John Ichabod."

"Er, yes." The clerk was about Troy's age and had big thick glasses. He opened a book and ran his finger down it. "Right. In a quarter of an hour."

"I like to be early," Troy said with a grin. "We'll wait."

"Right." The clerk nodded at Troy—then his eyes landed on Lola. And something happened that Troy had never seen happen to a man in real life before. His jaw dropped. He pulled himself together and smiled charmingly—which, Troy thought, was a feat for someone with glasses. "Is this lady your sister?"

Troy made a noise resembling a growl. He wasn't quite sure where it had come from, but it'd come nevertheless. "None of your business."

Yet Lola's eyes reflected curiosity. "I am his sister."

The clerk glanced up at Troy then back at Lola. "What's your name, Miss Kee?"

His fists clenched. "Her name is 'Seventeen And You'd Better Stay Away From Her.'"

The clerk laughed, entirely at ease despite the fact that Troy was trying to glare daggers at him. The cheek! "No disrespect meant, Mr. Kee, and she doesn't need to reply to me."

"Nor will she," Troy countered.

Lola placed a hand on his arm. "It's all right, Troy. My name is Eloise. And yours is?"

Troy gawked at his baby sister in astonishment. He supposed it was like Lola to give a stranger her name, but the odd little twinkle in her eye was new, as was that soft smile. What on earth was going on? She was still a baby. She'd better not have developed a crush-at-first-sight. Those were the worse kinds.

"I'm David Cole, though everyone calls me Dave, almost like my name isn't David, so perhaps you ought to, too." He smiled at her again, all charm. Honestly. Would this little bank clerk not back off?

Lola giggled. "All right, I will. And you should call me Lola. Everyone does."

"How sweet! I like that."

"You … you don't think it's silly?" The hesitance in his sister's voice made Troy realize he'd perhaps been a bit too annoying with his teasing.

"No, not at all! I think it's pretty. A lovely name."

Lola beamed, and Troy felt an ugly feeling sneaking into his gut. His sister and the clerk chatted incessantly the entire time they waited for Troy to have his meeting—and as far as he knew the whole time he was meeting with the bank manager.

It was only with the realization that Lola should not know their financial situation that he left her alone, but thankfully the meeting was not too lengthy, and she hadn't run off with the man when he returned.

Because Lola was Lola and apparently quite smitten with this arrogant clerk, she'd asked him to have dinner with them. Not only was that forward—Troy scolded her mightily for that—but it was stupid. He didn't ever want Lola to see Dave Cole again. Never. He had enough problems without his sister falling in love with some random bank clerk.

In the end, Troy managed to secure his loan—but he left that bank wishing he'd never brought Lola to England.

~

Troy told himself throughout the entire dinner that it was ridiculous. Lola was just having a bit of a crush on an older man—older by two years, anyway—and it would fade. These things always did.

Lola would come back to him and stop gazing across the table at this Dave Cole like he was something special instead of a thick-spectacled bank clerk who probably would never make a thing of himself or be able to provide for anyone.

And, Troy reasoned, *she loved me first!*

The sensible side of Troy told him that he wouldn't be able to compete with this sort of love, though—and when his sensible side started talking about emotions, he'd better listen.

A part of Troy knew that if he did lose her to another man, the loss would be complete. Women didn't get married and then live with their brothers.

Dave Cole was at least intelligent, and he seemed generally interested in Lola, as well as open about his own life. He was an only child, had two adoring parents, had moved out of their home in London about a year ago, and now resided in an apartment with three of his former schoolmates. Yes, he was a Christian. Church of England, of course, and had been all his life.

"I don't care about that," Lola said, surprising Troy.

He glared at his little sister. "What do you mean?" Of course it would be important that anyone Lola associated with was a Christian, too. Troy's faith wasn't anywhere near as strong as Lola's, but he still held to that .

She blushed and glanced down at her plate. "I don't care what your religion is. My mother was Catholic, my father Protestant, but it didn't matter. That was just how they were raised. What I want to know, Mr. Cole, is do you love the Lord? Are you one of His followers?"

And, confound him, Mr. Cole looked her right in the eyes and said, "Yes, I am. As I had hoped you are. I assume you go to church in France? Is that difficult?"

"It was at first," Lola said. "We both understand French perfectly, so that wasn't the problem—it was more finding a non-Catholic church. But there's one not far from where we live, so that worked out in the end. Troy doesn't always go, though." She elbowed him in the stomach.

Troy chuckled. "I'm just not one for people like Lola is. I can worship God by myself."

"Yes, but that's not the point." Lola glared at him for a minute then returned to the oh-so-fascinating Dave Cole.

Troy stabbed his salad through the heart and chewed it viciously. He was just about done with his sister having any interest in this random man who she'd just met.

Chapter Three

Spring 1928
London, England

Adele bit her lips nervously and turned in the mirror. She was dressed in the first real evening gown she'd ever owned, purchased with money carefully saved from months of work. Her saleswoman salary had groaned under the unnecessary expense, but it was worth it.

"What do you think?" She whirled to Millie who sat on the bed behind her.

"You look … daring," Millie said, swallowing hard. She always swallowed when she didn't want to insult Adele with her conservative opinions and yet felt honor-bound to state them. She also played with her glasses—pushing them up on her nose, down on her nose, and taking them off to polish them.

"That's the point, dear."

"I know," Millie said. She closed her eyes and recited the next part in a rush: "I don't think you should dress like that."

Adele sighed. Millie was a sweet girl, and Adele loved her more than life itself, more than anything or anyone else in the world, but she just didn't understand. This was what Adele needed. This was what she lived for. The glamor, the thrill, the excitement.

"I know you feel that way," Adele said after a long moment of silence, "and if your morals bother you too much, you're always welcome to leave or ask me to. You don't have to stay with me. We don't have to room together."

Millie shook her head. "I love you."

And that said everything. Adele knew very well that Millie would never willingly leave someone she loved, no matter how bad their sins were in her eyes. She imagined it could become somewhat of a problem if she ever did anything seriously wrong, but for now, she was just glad Millie was sticking with her. She needed a friend.

"But you hardly know him," Millie said seriously. "I don't see the point in dating if you're not going to be seriously committed."

"Oh, come now, Millie, don't be Victorian. I'm not entering into a courtship." Adele laughed at the very idea. "I'm just going out to dinner with a very fine, very handsome man. And I refused twice before I agreed to go."

"But you did agree to go!" Millie exclaimed. "Adele, I'm worried."

"Don't be! I can take care of myself, dear!" Millie was just having a case of the sympathetic nerves, Adele told herself. *She* wasn't nervous. Not one little bit. She was breaking away from the dowdy, old-fashioned girls she'd grown up with, the serious, hard-working boys, and their stolid, clingy parents.

She was sick and tired of being a lady. Tonight she could be who she wanted to be—Adele Collier, modern woman, going on a date with no strings attached … especially not strings attached to some grandmother's purse. She was through with all that.

"I'll be back before midnight. I promise."

Millie's eyebrows arched. "That's rather late, isn't it?"

Adele sighed. "You don't quite grasp the concept, do you, Millie? This is about getting out there. This is about taking risks. This is about, well, actually living for once in my miserable nineteen years."

Millie didn't reply.

"Please don't worry." Adele pulled her friend into a brief hug. "I've got it all under control. I'll be safe. We're going to dinner and then dancing. It's harmless."

Millie just sighed and shook her head slowly.

~

Adele was enjoying her date immensely. Edward Holly was turning out to be a wonderful gentleman, just as charming and clever as she'd come to believe when they'd met at the department store a few days ago.

It had really been a fluke, their meeting. He'd come to collect his younger sister, Jennifer, whom Adele happened to be helping. Edward had swaggered into the ladies' department, not looking as flustered as other men would have in his situation, suave and sophisticated. His hat had been cocked jauntily to the side, and, from his left hand, he listlessly swung a cane that he didn't seem to need.

Walking up to Adele and Jennifer, who were discussing the merits of a certain dress, he'd said, "Sis, I've been waiting in the car for half an hour now. 'Just looking' shouldn't require quite so much time. But I'll forgive you if you'll introduce me to your lovely friend here."

"Oh!" Jennifer had exclaimed. "She's not exactly my friend, Edward. I mean …" Jenny had blushed here. "We've only just met. But I do hope we can be friends, Adele." The fact that they were on a first-name basis proved that clothing brought women together.

"Of course we'll be friends!" Adele had exclaimed, laughing. "Anyone with such wonderful taste in clothes would have to be my friend."

"So …" Edward let his voice trail off and raised his eyebrows at his sister.

"Oh, of course! Adele, this is my brother, Edward Holly. Edward, my new friend, Adele Collier."

He grinned and shook her hand. "Pleasure to meet you. I hope my sister hasn't broken the bank?"

Adele shook her head. "Not that I know of. She's made a few purchases, but then she had to have a spring suit."

Edward laughed. "Well, then, if she *had* to have them. Now, let's go, Jenny. We've got that party tonight, and I promised you could tag along …"

"Oh, I'd forgotten! I'll just fetch my purse from the dressing room." She dashed off.

"Energetic kid, isn't she?" Edward cocked his head in his sister's direction.

"Yes, indeed," Adele had replied. "Probably a bit of a handful. She's about sixteen?"

"Just barely. Keeps me on my toes." He shrugged. "She's my only family, so it's no problem. Most of the time," he'd added laughingly.

From his clothes and the price tags his sister didn't bat an eye at, Adele had known then they were wealthy. He was handsome, agreeable, and seemed to genuinely care about his sister. And Adele was looking for someone handsome, agreeable, and caring to have a good time with.

So she had flirted shamelessly, and he'd ended up getting her number. A few days of persistent phone calls had worn her down—though she hadn't honestly had any resistance to begin with—and so here she was. Having dinner at a fancy club with a handsome man beaming at her from across the table.

She wasn't looking for anything serious. She'd been reminding herself of that all evening. That wasn't what modern women nowadays did—they had their own lives, and romance was in a separate field entirely—and she wanted so badly to be a modern woman. She craved it. She searched for every opportunity to be it. She just had to get into the right crowd, the kind of people who were interesting and independent.

"Adele?" Edward's voice cut through her thoughts. She blinked.

"Oh … sorry. Lost in thought," Adele said with a nervous giggle.

He smiled. “That’s all right. I was just making small talk.” He leaned forward conspiratorially. “I was falling asleep myself.”

She laughed. “Well, perhaps you should attempt to speak of something more interesting,” she suggested, raising her eyebrows archly.

He pretended to be offended. “Why, Miss Collier! Are you inferring that I’m a less-than-interesting conversationalist?” he demanded.

“You inferred it first!” Adele protested.

Edward laid a hand over his chest. “But of course! I was trying to distract you from your … shall we say less than perfect manners? Drifting off while I’m trying to talk to you shows an incredible lack of respect … of common decency, even!” Then his serious facade dropped. “Really, though, we should talk of something more amusing. I’m not used to boring first dates. It’s just not *me*.”

“You think it’s been boring?” Adele asked, a little hurt. She, for one, had been enjoying herself greatly.

“Well, no, actually. It’s been rather fun. But I don’t even allow for boring minutes. No, seconds! Boring moments are, in fact, absolutely forbidden for my first date … and every other date to follow.”

“I’d like to live a life where there are no boring moments,” said Adele.

“Well,” said Edward, “perhaps you shall.”

~

Adele’s life after that first date was anything but boring. Life became one huge party, and she was the belle of the ball.

Edward took her to different events, fancy dinners, and the movies. And she let herself grow attached to him—to fall under the spell of a charming smile and debonair attitude.

But she soon found that what to her had been a blossoming romance was to Edward nothing but a fun fling with an innocent girl. He informed her they wouldn't be seeing each other anymore after a few months of gaiety.

There were several days of depression on Adele's end, but she quickly caught on. Women didn't act hurt when someone broke their hearts. They acted even merrier. They danced, partied, laughed, and drank until they couldn't think anymore. No matter what, they didn't let anyone know they were hurting.

She told herself Edward had never meant anything to her anyway.

Hurt was old-fashioned. It was for a time everyone wanted to forget, for a war that made all wars before it seem tame. Now was the era of glamor. Pain gilded over with sparkly jewels.

She loved this life of hers. It thrilled her, and she felt truly herself for the first time since childhood. But Millie's eyes were worried and Adele's relationship with her mother nonexistent. All her old friends averted their eyes when she passed them on the street. If this is what modernity cost, she told herself she didn't care.

Chapter Four

Autumn 1929
French Riviera

Lola squealed as Dave chased her out amongst the whitecaps at the beach, and she splashed an insignificant amount of water his way. Troy grumpily pulled his knees up to his chest and glared at them.

He sat on a towel with a picnic lunch. Harrington had brought a chair down which he sat on as he read a book. Good old Harrington. At least someone around here still had some sense. Harrington didn't approve of Dave Cole any more than Troy did.

"It's not exactly that I mind that Lola has a friend," Troy began.

"Except you do." Harrington shot him a look over the top of his thick novel. "You mind very much."

"Yes, well." Troy shrugged. "It's not easy, and we don't know much about the man."

In the past year and a half, Dave Cole had become a big part of Lola's life. He seemed to ring them up every day, write letters every hour, and he was always trying to talk Lola into coming to see him.

Twice, he'd succeeded. Once with Troy, once without. The time she'd gone without him, she'd met Mr. and Mrs. Cole. Troy still winced at the idea of this. Meeting a boyfriend's parents had to be some sort of landmark for a young woman. It meant she was serious. That she was sticking around, and Mr. and Mrs. Cole had better take notice of it. Troy didn't like that one bit.

At last Lola ran up and wrapped a towel around herself, skin flushed and hair springing every which way.

"Dave's incorrigible," she said to no one in particular. "He dunked me under the water, and now I'll have frizzy hair all day!"

"I like it frizzy." Dave dropped onto the blanket next to her. "You look lovely."

Lola blushed and laughed and told him he was full of nonsense, but she secretly liked his compliments. Troy could tell. That drove him even madder.

Why did Dave have to come visit them on holiday? Why had he let Lola talk him into it? Why did he love his sister so much that he had to give her everything she wanted—and therefore stood to lose her in the process?

It just wasn't fair.

Eventually Lola went off to dry her hair and clean up a bit before they ate their picnic lunch. Harrington followed her, already tired of the sun and sand. He might live on the Riviera, but he preferred to stay in his nice cool rooms.

“I’m glad I’ve got a moment alone with you,” said Dave.

Troy blinked at him. “If you knew what’s going through my head right now, you wouldn’t be.” He’d considered murder at several points, and he thought he might be able to twist the bank clerk’s head off and throw him into the sea before Lola returned.

But that would break her heart, which was unthinkable.

Dave just chuckled. “I can understand that. I don’t have a sister, but I believe if I did, I’d be protective of her. There’s nothing wrong with that.” He shrugged and rubbed the seawater and sand off his glasses with the blanket edge. “But I suppose you know what I want to ask you.”

“Don’t bother.”

Dave seemed to think this was a big joke, for he laughed again. He was always laughing, always light-hearted. What did Lola see in him? She’d certainly not been raised around laughing, light-hearted men. It was so contrary to what she was used to. “Well, I want to ask your permission to marry your sister. I know you’re the closest thing to a father she has, and I want to do this thing right. I haven’t spoken to her about it, but she knows, of course.” He took a deep breath. “I can provide for her. I’ll be a banker all my life, I think, and that’s not a bad job. Pays well. We’d live in London, of course—I have a place picked out. I know we’re both young, but we’ll have my parents’ counsel, and we love each other very much.”

Troy stared at him wordlessly.

“Well? What do you say?”

“No.”

Dave stared at him for about thirty painfully long seconds then broke out into a laugh that was nervous but still fairly unconvinced that Troy meant it.

"No, I'm serious. You can't marry her. She's too young." Eighteen was not old enough to enter into a serious relationship with a man she'd only known a year and a half. It was too young, too sweet, too personal.

Dave cocked his head. "You mean *you're* not ready. Not ready to give up your sister. And I can understand that, but—"

"Translate it how you will. *No, non, nein*." Troy stood and stomped off, up the hill toward the vineyard. He passed Lola toward the top.

"What is it?" she asked.

"Let's go home."

"What? No! We're going to finish our picnic." She grabbed his arm. "Troy?" Her face was full of curiosity and worry.

"You're not going to marry him!" he burst out. "Not now, not later, not ever!"

Lola stood there for a second, lips pursed, then smiled up at him. Her hand trembled on his arm, but her voice was firm. "Troy, did it occur to you that I'm going to marry him whether you like it or not?"

Troy gulped. "You can't."

"I can and I will!" She took a deep breath. "He's the man I love, Troy. I'm not giving him up easily. Look at me! I'm eighteen now. I'll be nineteen in a few months. You may be the most important man in my world besides him, but there are things I won't do for you—and reject the man I love and remain single forever are some of those things." Lola placed her hands on her hips. "You're just going to have to get used to it, Troy. I'm putting my foot down on this. So you march right back to that picnic and tell him he can have my hand in marriage. Now. I mean it."

Troy stared her down, but she didn't flinch. She didn't even blink. She just stared back at him, a strange mixture of fierce and appealing. He looked away first.

"Fine," he mumbled. "Fine."

Lola softened a bit. "He'll make me very happy, you know."

"Whatever."

"I love him."

A low growl was all he managed.

She stood on tiptoes to kiss his cheek then gave him a gentle shove back toward the picnic. "I'll be out in a minute, dear."

~

Lola and Dave married a few months later. It helped ease it down Troy's throat that Lola was ecstatically happy, but he still wanted to gag from time to time.

He didn't want his sister to leave him. To go to England, so far away. He wanted her to be safe with him—not off in London with Dave Cole. Who knew what could happen to her now that he wasn't nearby?

Everything in him revolted at the unnatural displacement of his sister from his side. It was like someone had cut off a piece of his heart and thrown it countries away.

He sent her off on her honeymoon, went out onto

the vineyard grounds, and sat down on a rock far above the cliff that overlooked the Mediterranean.

He sat there for hours, just thinking.

Hoping that someday his life without Lola would be complete. That he wouldn't be alone. That he would have someone to count on, and someone who counted on him.

A family.

Chapter Five

Winter 1929
London, England

"Adele?" Something soft hit her over the head. "Adele, if you stay in bed a minute longer, we'll be late!"

Adele moaned and waved her hand in the direction of Millie's voice. "I changed my mind. I want to sleep in."

"A*dele*!" Millie stressed both syllables of her best friend's name. "You promised! Please? It … it means a lot to me."

At last Adele pushed herself up to a sitting position and yawned. "All right, all right! I'm coming. Do I have time to wash up first?"

Millie smiled. "Yes, you have plenty of time to wash up. I've picked out a nice, *conservative* dress for you to wear, too! And I've decided on the amount of makeup you can wear to look pretty but not like a dance-hall girl. And—"

"Oh, gracious, Millie, you're so concerned about what people think." Adele swung her legs over the edge of the bed and stumbled her way to the bathroom.

It was true, though. Millie liked to be a nice proper little English girl with a nice proper womanly job who went to church every Sunday and never danced or flirted or drank or smoked.

Adele, on the other hand, hadn't stepped in a church since she arrived in London. However, Millie had finally wore her down, so here she was—washing her face and dabbing on a bit of powder and no lipstick, putting on a sweet conservative dress and shoes without six-inch heels.

Her hat was also a plain straw one, and she wore no flashy jewelry—though she couldn't resist a simple pearl necklace. But pearls were all right; they were modest and church-like. Even her mother wore pearls to church.

"You look very nice," said Millie with an approving nod. She wore an even more conservative dress than Adele—but Millie was always dressed like that. It was just her style. *Honestly,* Adele thought, *she's almost dowdy sometimes.*

But Millie was a pretty girl, from the rims of her spectacles to the dress that hung two inches too low for current fashions to her black flats. She just didn't try.

They walked to the Episcopal church nearby. The building mostly seemed to contain folks aged forty and older with a scattering of "younger" ones in their mid-30s.

They took a seat in the very back of the church. The singing had already started, but Millie opened a hymnal and pointed to the correct song. Of course she did. Millie was perfect like that.

Adele admitted to being somewhat unfamiliar with the tune, but she sang as best she could, softly under her breath. She figured it was the respectful thing to do what with Millie being so convinced this was so important to Adele's salvation or whatever it was.

She also remained attentive and quiet through a sermon that didn't begin to make sense to her. Millie seemed to like it, but Adele supposed that ought to be assumed. After all, Millie was a Christian, and Christians should enjoy church.

There were a few things the pastor said that made Adele rather uncomfortable. Words about repentance and Heaven and Hell and sin and Satan. She didn't want to go to Hell, but neither was she willing to 'repent.'

Nothing she'd done was really bad, anyway. Her mother might call her a demon on occasion, but that was only because she didn't understand her. Besides, demon wasn't the right term. Even Adele knew that.

But she didn't feel like a sinner, either, and she didn't need anyone, especially God. It was her against the world. That is, with Millie's occasional help.

At last the service was over. Adele breathed a heavy sigh of relief as the last hymn ended, and they were released back into the real world.

She hastened toward the door, but Millie caught her arm.

"Part of it is actually staying and talking to people," she said sternly, and Adele didn't dare disobey her. She just meekly stood next to Millie while about five thousand people greeted her, inquired politely after her friend, and moved on.

At last the torture ended, and the two walked home in peace.

It had gone so well that Adele let herself be talked into coming again the following week. That time she was able to relax a bit more, actually listen, actually hear the words of the songs and in the sermon.

It was all quite interesting, really. Because she was an adult, she felt more inclined to listen than she had as a girl forced to go to church by her mother. After all, if it was self-inflicted, she might as well get something out of it, even if it was just confirmation that her beliefs were the right ones and Christianity was a big sham.

When the sermon was over, Millie slid off to use the restroom while Adele waited just outside the church. A group of women approached her.

There were four or five of them, all similarly dressed in simple conservative outfits with big going-to-church hats covered in flowers. They must have all been in their 40s, too, if Adele were any judge of age.

They marched up to Adele, and the ring-leader, the one in the front, addressed her.

"You!" She frowned. "You're Millie's friend, aren't you? Adele Collier?"

Adele gulped but smiled bravely. "Yes, that's me. And you are—"

“None of your business, you arrogant hussy!” The woman snorted. “How dare you, you filthy wolf in sheep’s clothing! How dare you come to our church acting like one of us when really … well! I can’t believe it.”

“What exactly can’t you believe?” Adele asked calmly. She had a good idea that somehow the women had found out about the parties, the drinking, the men, and were calling her out for it. Though she didn’t know why. It wasn’t like it was any of their business.

“That a filthy woman like you would dare set foot in God’s house.”

Adele blinked. “Would you care to explain that blanket statement a bit?”

The woman snorted and glared at Adele. “You surely know what you’ve done! We’ve heard about you. It wasn’t hard to find out—the way you spread your filth all over town. You—”

“What have I done?” Adele wasn’t sure if she was taunting or curious as to which of the golden rules she’d broken to incur such wrath.

“We know about your habits! A different man every night, dancing, drinking, out until all hours of the morning doing who knows what with who knows whom … we’ve heard stories that I wouldn’t dare repeat!”

“But you would listen to them,” Adele replied solemnly. “I think I’ve heard quite enough. I imagine I’m not welcome in your church?”

“Definitely not!” said one of the other women. There was a murmur of agreement.

"Very well, then. I'll wait for Millie before I leave."

The women practically growled in her direction. "Leading that poor sweet girl down the path to sin," one of them said. "Poor Millie!"

"Millie knows all that I do. And some of it isn't as bad as you have been led to believe. Yes, I date around—yes, I spend my evenings and nights at parties, and yes, I drink when I'm at those parties. But it's not like I'm sleeping around with whomever—"

Quiet gasps, and one of the women said, "That's quite enough! We don't need to hear about your filthy life."

"I'm just saying, it's not as filthy as—"

"Get out of here, you and your filthy life and your filthy mouth!" said the ring-leader. "We don't need your kind in God's holy house."

Adele wasn't sure why she flinched so hard. It hit her in a soft vulnerable place. God didn't want her, and certainly no one who believed in God would.

It's all right, she told herself as she walked away. *I don't care. I don't believe. His opinion doesn't matter to me, and neither do the opinions of those ladies.*

Yet a burning in her heart said otherwise. It did matter. Of course it mattered. People couldn't say such wretched things to anyone without heartbreak ensuing.

Yet she knew in her soul that her fate was sealed. She couldn't—she wouldn't—turn back now.

~

Adele was sitting on her bed staring at the wall when Millie arrived back at their apartment half an hour later.

"Adele! You worried me sick, walking off like that! I looked everywhere, and at last I guessed you must have come back home, but I almost had a heart attack worrying that you'd been kidnapped or … or who knows what!"

Adele didn't respond.

Millie sat on the bed opposite her. "Adele? What is it? Why did you leave?"

Adele blinked then slowly raised her eyes to Millie's face. "Nothing, Millie. It's nothing." She rose and walked into the kitchen rather stiffly, still not fully animated after those women had knocked the breath out of her.

"Nothing? Then … then why …?" Millie's voice trailed off. Adele turned to face her. She was standing there, eyes befuddled behind her thick glasses.

"It's all right, Millie. I mean it." Adele attempted a smile which she hoped was at least mildly convincing. "Don't worry. I just got tired of waiting and came home."

"Oh. All right. Well, I am sorry. I got distracted halfway back talking to a friend—and you know how talkative people are there."

Adele nodded. Indeed, she did know. They could talk and talk and use their words like swords or cannons. Piercing her flesh, causing an ache that wouldn't go away.

Yet she knew she couldn't heed the ache. She must go on pretending it didn't matter. At this point, she was plainly too far gone to turn back. At this point, she had been rejected by all that was good and holy.

She didn't understand it. She thought the bad girls were the ones who slept around or drank until they couldn't see straight.

Yes, Adele had boyfriends, but she'd never gone further than a few kisses—call it a personal standard or a desire to not go down that particular emotional rabbit trail. She didn't think she'd be able to bounce back from that as easily as the girls she saw around her.

And yes, she did drink, and a few times she'd become tipsy, but she'd never forgotten what had happened the previous night or done something unpardonably stupid—silly was as far as she'd gotten —so it seemed that that would be forgivable, too.

Yet it would seem that she was beyond pardon now. She couldn't show her face in church anymore. They knew her too well, had found out from the gossip mills that she was bad, and now she was banished from polite society or religion or whatever one wanted to call the church-going crowd.

"Are you sure you're all right?" Millie asked, drawing Adele back to the present moment.

Adele nodded, the wheels of her mind turning rapidly. There was such a thing as being infamous by association, and now that they knew what Adele was and that Millie was her friend … "Millie, I think we ought to live separately."

Millie blinked then shook her head firmly. "I don't know what's happened to you, Adele, but of course we can't! Why, neither of us can afford it—and you least of all with all your expenses."

It was true that Adele loved pretty dresses, expensive makeup, having her nails done, perfumes, and all other sorts of things that took sizable amounts away from her monthly paychecks. However, she'd have to figure a way around it. She couldn't hurt Millie—that would be the straw that broke the camel's back.

"But don't you think … don't you think … well, Millie, you're a Christian."

"Yes …" Millie's voice trailed off questioningly.

"And I'm not."

"Right. But what does that have to do—"

"I think I ought to move out. Why would a Christian like you want to be with someone like me? Even if you want to, well, witness or something like that, why live with me? We could talk sometimes, and I'll always love you, and I'll always be your friend, but isn't it unwise to associate with me? Isn't sin somewhat contagious?"

Millie's blinks became so rapid that Adele thought she might be on the verge of explosion, then they stopped all together. "Not that I've heard of, Adele. It's true that I want to witness to you. I want to witness to you every day by being a good and faithful friend, by loving you, by my loyalty, by seeing beyond your exterior to the Adele within, and by sharing my life with you. The biggest way I can witness to another person is by simply being a Christian—simply sharing their life, the beautiful joy that God has given me."

Adele shook her head. "Yes, but surely a Christian shouldn't spend time with a sinner."

Millie narrowed her eyes. "Did you get all this from that sermon? Yes, Pastor Jordan talked about repentance a great deal—he always seems to—but that's never affected you before. What happened?"

"Nothing. I just realized—"

Millie crossed the room and put her hands on Adele's arms. "Please. Tell me. I'm your best friend. Surely you can trust me."

"I … I don't want to gossip."

Millie smiled. "Isn't that what best friends are for?"

Adele let out a tight chuckle. "Yes, I suppose so. Well … while you were gone, a group of ladies came up to me."

"Oh! I didn't think of that." Millie's posture deflated. "I know who you're talking about without you telling me. Well, go on. What did they say to you? Horrific things, I imagine?"

Adele nodded. "Only that I was a wicked, terrible girl, that I was immoral, and that I was never welcome at their church."

Millie moaned softly, surprising even Adele. "They didn't! How terrible of them."

"Yes, well, they spoke rather truthfully. You know I've kept a lot of the rules just because I don't think sleeping around is safe for me—emotionally or physically—and I don't know that I want to become quite so stupid as most people become when drunk. I haven't taken any other horrid things, but … still. I know I walk a tightrope, and I know it must seem to others that I'm breaking every commandment as thoroughly as I can."

"It … it can be hard to judge exactly what you're at, Adele," Millie admitted. "And, yes, I admit to myself that taking you to that particular church was a bad idea. They're … they're good people, Adele. Truly they are. They just … they are all from a generation that isn't used to this sort of thing, and they weren't raised to understand how to act around people who weren't Christians." She tilted her head and gazed worriedly at Adele. "They weren't right, but they didn't know any better."

"But that doesn't change the fact that you could be shunned because of me! And you don't want that."

Millie wrapped Adele in a tight hug. "It's all right, dearest. I don't care. I don't care one bit! Of course, I want you to be the best Adele you can be—but I won't reject you. I still love you. I suppose you could say I'm not that sort of Christian!" She took a deep breath. "I don't suppose any Christian should reject their friend over something like this. Regardless, I know I won't."

Adele just stood there for a moment, her face in Millie's shoulder, and let herself be held and tried not to cry despite the tightness in her throat and the heaving in her chest.

It was nice to know it wasn't just Adele against the world. It was nice to know … to know that someone really cared. Really would stand by her through thick and through thin despite her choices, bad or good or morally gray.

"I love you, too, Millie. You're a fantastic friend, you know," Adele whispered.

Millie laughed softly. "Thanks. I try." She drew back and looked Adele in the eye. "So don't you go running off on me, Adele Collier! You're the best friend I've got, and about the only thing that keeps me from losing this apartment sometimes and running home to my mama. Besides, I need someone to talk to and cry and giggle with … and talk about Jane Austen!"

Adele laughed. It turned into a bit of a hiccup that sounded suspiciously like a sob, but Millie pretended not to notice even if she had.

"Do you understand me?" Millie asked. She had her hands on her hips and her head cocked, her "mother knows best" expression on her face.

"Yes. Yes, I understand you," Adele said meekly. "No more talk about moving out. I'm sticking with you, Millie."

"Good!" Millie took her apron off a hook and tied it around her slim waist. It was a cute pink one with ruffles that Adele thought looked adorable on her best friend.

Honestly, the girl looked like a little housewife! Adele hoped Millie would find someone soon, though goodness knows she wasn't willing to let Adele set her up with any men she knew.

If Adele were honest, she'd admit that she agreed with Millie. Her best friend was too sweet, too innocent, too pure to be sullied by any company Adele kept.

Chapter Six

Summer 1930
French Riviera

Troy had an afternoon off, and it hardly seemed fair. He'd done everything there was possible to do, and now there was nothing left, so he sat in the baking hot sun, staring at the blue waves rippling off toward the horizon and trying not to consider self-harm as a means of entertainment.

Harrington was no help. On the hottest days of the year, he locked himself in his bedroom with all the shades drawn and slept half the day. Besides, even when he was awake, he didn't want to talk.

Troy thought he was going mad.

He needed a companion. Someone to talk to and share life with. Someone who would always be there for him …

He needed a good dog.

Troy had never been allowed to have a dog as a child. There just wasn't room for one in their house, nor could they always afford another hungry mouth. But now there was plenty of room for a dog, and he could probably afford to keep a puppy on scraps and bones or whatever it was that dogs ate.

Troy rose from his bench which overlooked the Mediterranean and walked back to the house. When he arrived, he went straight to the telephone and picked up the receiver.

Then he set it down, realizing that telephoning for a dog was about the most ridiculous thing he'd ever tried to do.

He picked up the receiver again and called the one person he knew would know everything going on in the nearby town—Madame Bernard.

"Madame Bernard? It's Troy Kee," he said in French.

"*Bonjour*, Troy! What can I help you with today?"

"Well, it's not groceries I'm after, Madame Bernard." Troy took a deep breath. "I'm actually looking for a puppy."

Madame Bernard laughed. "I'm afraid we don't sell puppies here, Troy."

"*Oui*, but … I thought if anyone knew where a litter was to be had, it would be you, madame. So do you know of one?"

"I know of three," the woman admitted.

Troy had to chuckle. Besides the gossip, Madame Bernard was also informed about world matters and had a kind of common sense wisdom that Troy appreciated. Especially in regards to women. He was rather clueless in that area, but she'd taught him to sit still and listen and try to understand, and for that, he would be eternally thankful.

"The first belongs to a little boy down the street from me—they're about ready to go home now. He brought me one to see, and it was a sweet little pup!"

"What kind?" Troy asked. He didn't know much about dogs, and doubted he'd be able to form a mental image when he heard the breed, but he felt that that was the sort of question one asked about a dog.

"A mixed breed. Some hound in it, I think. It had a speckled nose that was quite sweet! And the oddest long ears."

"And the other two litters?"

"One is young, born only a week ago," the woman continued. "They're poodles. I don't think you'd like a poodle, now, would you, Troy?"

Troy shook his head and cleared his throat. "I think we can steer away from those. Poodles are just … well, if I ever had a baby girl"—*not that I ever would*—"I'd want her to have a poodle, but I'd never own one by myself."

"I thought not." He could hear the smile in her voice. "And the last litter is somewhere between the other two in age. You'd have to wait a few weeks to take one home, I imagine."

"What type?" he asked again.

"Funny little black dogs. I'm not sure what. Some kind of terrier. A lady in her final years owns the mother, and the father—well, who knows."

"All right, then. I think the first would be the ones if any, though I'll visit the terriers, too. Can you give me the addresses?"

"*Oui*. Do you have a paper?"

"Yes."

Madame Bernard rattled them off, and Troy wrote them down.

"*Merci*. I'll let you know which I bring home," Troy said. "I don't know that I will just yet—I think this is a decision not to be taken lightly, since I'll have the dog for the next ten or fifteen years—so I might wait around for a few months and see what comes up. You'll keep me informed, *oui*?"

"*Oui*," said Madame Bernard, "and if you're looking for a dog, Troy, I can think of half a dozen who'd be happy to give theirs away! Especially to a good home, and I know you'd give a dog a good home."

"I've never had a dog before, Madame Bernard," Troy admitted.

Madame Bernard chuckled. "Yes, but you'd be a good owner! I can tell these things. You're kind, and you take time with things."

Troy wasn't so sure about that—he didn't feel kind or patient a lot of the time now—but he nodded to himself. "All right then. I'll be sure to let you know if I don't choose one of the puppies." He doubted he would—he had a very specific if somewhat idealistic idea of the dog he wanted, and he wouldn't settle for anything else.

"*Oui*. I'll see you then," said Madame Bernard.

Troy hung up and examined the slip of paper he'd written the addresses on. He'd walk down to the village to visit them today.

~

Frustration filled Troy's chest as he left the elderly lady's house. The terriers hadn't been any better than the hound mixes.

Granted, there wasn't a thing wrong with the puppies, except that they just weren't right. Something about them made him hesitate. He needed the puppy to be absolutely perfect—yet the sense of overwhelming perfection wasn't coming to him.

It wasn't something he could put into words—a gut instinct. He knew none of these puppies would turn into the perfect dog. So, he thanked the owners for showing him the pups, but he didn't think he'd be taking one.

The next logical step was to visit Madame Bernard and ask about the grown dogs and half-grown pups that people wanted to give away, but he'd really wanted to raise the dog from a whelp. It made more sense having it be his from the start.

Besides, grown dogs weren't nearly as adorable. And he might be a man, but that didn't mean he didn't want to own the most adorable puppy in the world.

He trudged away from the village and up the hill. The Martel vineyards overlooked the town, of course, which was nice as far as scenery went—there were multiple places where one could view the sea, the beaches, and the stretch of cottages along it—but it was rather hard to get home.

Of course, walking down when one wasn't hot, tired, and hungry was easier than walking up when one was. Oh, the unfairness of it all! He'd rather live in a valley with a town up on the hill. That would be so much easier to bear.

He was probably going to starve by the time he got home. They'd find his skeleton on the roadside and erect a marker. Lola would cry at his funeral. Harrington would look sad.

His gravestone would read, *Here lies Troy Kee. The road was too steep, the sun too hot, and the day too frustrating.*

Troy vowed to buy a car as soon as he had the money to do so. A shiny, fast silver car that would drive him up the hill in a whirl of dust. He'd be home in half the time, and wouldn't the drive be fun? He'd never owned a car, though Harrington had taught him to drive in a borrowed jalopy. However, he knew he'd enjoy driving—and he knew he'd drive fast.

He closed his eyes for a moment as he stood in the road before continuing his uphill trudge. He was just entering the vineyard grounds when he heard a soft whimpering coming from somewhere off the road a bit.

Troy stopped and looked around, trying to decide where the noise was coming from. At last he pinpointed the exact location—a small bush a short distance from him. He quickly closed the gap then hesitated.

It sounded like some sort of animal, but who knew if it were wild or not? Should he be more careful? What if it was something that could harm him—or what if he harmed it by disturbance?

At last he got up courage and lifted the trailing branch of the bush. Underneath was a little nest of sorts—more of a hollow lined with a bit of fur—and in the hollow lay a puppy.

It was about the same size as the four-week-old

terrier pups he'd seen earlier, but its tightly closed eyes and laid back ears told him it was younger.

"Hello, little fellow—or lady," he said softly. Then he realized it was a French dog and repeated his words in French. Then he realized that dogs of this age couldn't hear at all and inwardly berated himself.

"Well. I wonder where his mother is." Troy glanced about, but no mother dog appeared. He stood. "She must be coming back soon, and I have to get home for dinner."

Yet his conscience twinged. He shouldn't leave such a little thing by itself, alone and able to be taken down by the elements, by wild animals, by other dogs. It was defenseless. What if its mother was gone?

I'll just have to stay and see if she comes back. He crossed the road and took a seat on a rock where he could watch.

He waited and waited, but no one came to claim the pup. The sun dipped below the horizon, and still he waited. It began to grow black. The pup's intermittent cries were weak now. Troy could barely hear them. They sounded so sad and desperate.

At last, Troy stood and crossed the road again. Reaching under the bush, he put his hand on the puppy. The poor thing was so still and stiff. Swiftly, he lifted it, although it made some raspy protesting noises, and rubbed it with his hands.

He's painfully small. Troy double-checked then. *At least I know it's a* he. *That's something gained.*

Troy tucked the puppy in his pocket and began the walk back home. He didn't know who it belonged to—someone might claim it eventually, he supposed, but until then, he'd do his best to raise the little fellow.

When he arrived back home, he went straight to the kitchen and withdrew the puppy from his pocket. It shuddered and made a soft squeaking noise.

"That's all right. Don't worry. I've got you, boy." He found a towel, laid it on the table, and set the puppy on top. He was a funny looking little thing with no eyes, and the flaps that were his ears laid back against his head. He was a yellowish color with black splotches on his back and little whip of a tail.

"What do you have there?" Harrington rose from the kitchen table. "And what kept you so long?"

"Don't tell me you worried," Troy said, gently rubbing the puppy's back.

"No, but I wondered. I imagine the delay was in finding that puppy? Isn't he rather young to take home?"

Troy shrugged. "Found him on the road."

"Oh. Well, did you think that maybe his mother had left him for a bit?" Harrington asked. "Maybe you should take him back."

"No, I waited there for hours. The pup's weak with hunger and cold, and I didn't want to leave him there."

Harrington shrugged and left the kitchen. Troy opened the icebox and began searching for some milk.

After some trial and error, Troy found out how to feed and care for the puppy. He got up multiple times every night to make sure he wasn't cold or hungry or even just lonely.

And, over the days, Troy became determined to keep the puppy for his own.

He started calling the puppy Holt because he thought that sounded just like him—rugged and simple. Harrington seemed generally disgusted with him, but Troy insisted upon the name.

Holt was his and his alone.

Chapter Seven

November 1930
London, England

Adele's newest beau was Darcy James. Darce was a dashing gentleman—more charming than any of her other boyfriends. If Adele were honest with herself, that charm made him more dangerous, but she wasn't being honest with herself just then.

Honesty was overrated anyway.

All that mattered was that Darce took her on dates to the finest restaurants, bought her expensive gifts, and didn't seem to be looking for anything serious. Not that any of her other boyfriends had been, but she strictly adhered to these requirements.

If her heart became involved, it wouldn't be just Adele anymore. It'd be Adele and her boyfriend or Adele and her husband, should such a thing come to pass. And she couldn't—she just couldn't.

There wasn't a man in the world she could trust as far as she could throw them—and given the fact that she was 5'1" and attempted to weigh less with every day that passed, that wasn't very far.

It was a chilly late autumn night when Darce took her to a fancy club. Being above her budget, she'd never been there before—Darce was well-off, it would seem.

He handed her a small rectangular box. "Just something I picked up on the way over, love." He winked at her as she took it. She opened it and gasped when a diamond necklace sparkled in the light from the crystal chandeliers.

"Thought you didn't have anything like that."

Adele's hand went automatically to the double string of pearls around her neck. She had a few things, but none quite so expensive. "No, I don't, Darce," she whispered. "Nothing like this."

"Run to the powder room and try it on." He leaned back in his chair. "I'm sure it will go well with your dress."

It would indeed. He had thought ahead—how could he have known what she was going to wear? But the necklace would no doubt go with any number of things. Still, she shook her head. "It's too spendy for me, Darce. I can't. I'm sorry, but I just …"

She couldn't explain why she felt a need to turn down his gift. It was something in the depths of her stomach that twisted and told her not to. As if it were some kind of … of payment. Payment for what? Her mind couldn't bear to form the thought. She knew what other girls did—but had saved herself the final indignity. Something always stopped her.

She might not strictly adhere to morals, but she did know treating something important like nothing wasn't the way to go about life. It was careless and harsh, and she didn't want that. Even if it meant she couldn't accept the necklace.

"Oh, nonsense, love! I want to see it on you. Really. Go try it on."

Well—perhaps it was just like other little presents, only with his money Darce could afford to buy her something richer. It was like chocolate and flowers but from a very wealthy man. She took the necklace and went to try it on.

She came back beaming. It was truly the most marvelous thing she'd ever owned—if she could convince herself to keep it. Darce smiled languidly when she approached, swirling his champagne glass.

"Lovely," he said. "Are you ready to go?"

Adele hesitated, not liking the expression on his face. "Will we go dancing?"

"Dancing?" He chuckled. "Well, I have considered it, but don't you think there'd be a bit of a crowd this time of night? Let's go to my place."

"To … your place?" That was another thing Adele had never let herself do. She might occasionally let a man into her apartment to smoke and drink and kiss on the couch—but she'd never go to his place. It was an unspoken rule—and she'd made her boyfriends respect it even when they hadn't particularly wanted to.

In the past, Adele had been good at making men behave.

"Yes, of course. You want to see it, don't you? I've had it refurbished recently."

She knew very well that no man wanted a girl to admire his wallpaper. They always had separate motives—and that involved something she wasn't ready for.

Not yet. It had to be someone special. Darce wasn't that man—wasn't *the* man.

She didn't know that she believed in forever, but she did believe it ought to be a little less casual. She was going to have to be wooed into that step.

"No, Darce. I'm sorry," Adele said in a soft voice. "We can go to mine—or we can go walking—or we can go dancing. But I won't go to your place. And … I think you ought to know now that I don't really let men spend their nights with me."

His eyes grew cold. "Love. I take all my girls to my place. You can't expect special treatment."

Adele swallowed. "I know I can't *expect* it. But I will ask for it. Darce, I'm not ready. Perhaps, if we got to know each other …" There. She had held out an olive branch. He could take it or leave it as he chose.

He cussed. "I wouldn't have believed it of you."

"I know. Most men don't believe it." Adele clasped her hands in her lap and stared at the remains of her dinner, her half-empty champagne glass, the crumpled napkin on her plate. "I ask for a little respect is all. I just … I haven't been able to let myself …" She sighed and shook her head. "I suppose I still have a little of my mother in me."

His lips tightened. "I see. Well, I'll call you a cab, and you can make your own way home." He rose abruptly.

She followed him out of the restaurant. In no time, a cab was driving her swiftly back to her apartment.

Adele fought hard against the tears all the drive home, but they insisted on coming. She knew he would spread the word about their crowd. In no time at all, everyone would be aware that she was a child. A moralistic Victorian. A prude. They would shun her.

If only she had played hard to get with Darce as she had with all the other men—convincing them she slept around, just not with *them*. But somehow she had known that Darce wouldn't take no for an answer unless it was put in the form of an actual 'no,' not a teasing, flirtatious one.

She leaned back against the seat, closed her eyes, and wept, smothering her sobs into her handkerchief. She had gone too far to turn back now. There would be no redeeming her reputation.

She'd be firmly labeled a good girl now.

~

"Perhaps … perhaps you could give up this life," Millie said when Adele explained the situation to her.

Adele just laughed. "Millie. For goodness' sake. You know I can't! I love this life, and anyway, I don't know how to stop." She paused for a minute, troubled, then forced herself to go on with a smile. "I have ever so much fun. You'd be surprised, Millie! You should let yourself go out on date—have a nice dinner, maybe go dancing. Live a little. You're going to make yourself an old maid."

Millie shook her head. Adele wasn't sure, but she thought she saw a shudder wrench her body. "I'm afraid I'm just not interested. And, anyway, I wouldn't know how. But perhaps … I could help you stop, Adele. We could go to my parents' place in Kent for a few weeks, relax, take a break. We could avoid your mother and just stay at my house. I could easily get the time off—if not, I'll quit my job. You can refocus. Figure out what you want to do with your life. And then we can come back. Or not. We could always stay with my parents for an extended amount of time—"

Adele shook her head. "I'm not really interested."

The last people in the world she wanted to face were Millie's family members. Quiet as mice, all of them. Her father went for long walks and tended a garden; her mother stitched samplers and read. Her two younger sisters, from what Adele could tell, did very little with their lives.

They were all so upright. Moralistic. Kind and gentle. She didn't fear their judgment; she feared their goodness. They were such a perfectly godly family, and it frightened her.

"Very well, then." Millie sighed. "Adele, I want you to know that … I'm always praying for you. Always will be. I don't think it's too late. Why, the way you turned down Darcy James proves that! I just wish you'd—"

Adele held up her hand. "I don't want to talk about it."

"Very well," Millie said quietly. "But dearest—remember I am always here to talk if you want."

Adele loved Millie, so she gave her a quick hug and a smile. "I remember. I'm here for you, too, okay? Even if I don't always act like I am."

Millie nodded. "I know."

~

The day after Adele broke up with Darce, she was met with more bad news. A letter arrived from her Aunt Ella, who was Uncle Caleb's wife.

He'd died. At only fifty-six years old, of a stroke that no one could have predicted. She hadn't seen him since she was ten or eleven years old, and she was surprised Aunt Ella even remembered to write her.

She wasn't sure she was intensely sad, but she felt awful that she hadn't gone to visit him, and that she would never see him again. He'd been such a cheerful man, even in the face of her less-than-cheerful moments. She'd miss him.

The letter was kind, though. After a few paragraphs talking about the normal things one talked about when announcing a death and celebrating a life, Aunt Ella's letter became very interesting indeed.

> *Which brings me to one of the principle reasons I decided to write this letter. Your uncle and I ended our lives with a bit of a fortune from various avenues, which we worked hard to maintain and expand.*
>
> *I'm well-provided for and always shall be. But Caleb wanted us to decide together where the money would go, so we'd worked something out in case something happened to either of us. Granted, we were thinking a car accident or*

something, not this, but the will still stands.

Mostly, we've benefited various nieces, and we decided to include you. Caleb thought you could make good use of money, if you were smart about it. We decided to bequeath you the amount of £2,000, which should be enough to give you a solid foundation in whatever you choose to pursue without, as your Uncle Caleb would say, absolutely spoiling you.

Our lawyers will take care of the details, but I wanted to write you a personal note. As for me, a great many people have been worrying about me lately, and I am heartily sick of it. I'm quite well, for I know my husband is resting in God's arms, and I look forward to meeting him again some day in Heaven. Until then, I am content to do what I can here on earth.

God keep you,
Mrs. Ella Knight

~

It was then, on the strength of a rebound and with her Uncle Caleb's fortune, that Adele decided to open a flower shop. A recently empty building sat across the street from their apartment. It had just two little rooms—one for storage, one for display—and a big picture window at the front with a glass case.

She had passed it every day on the way to work, and it had filled her with all sorts of ideas. But her favorite was always turning it into a flower shop.

Flowers, to Adele, were the epiphany of beauty and romance. She had enjoyed receiving them, picking them, and arranging them since she was a small girl.

Millie had business sense, and Adele knew if she could get her to agree to the project, it would become more than a simple daydream.

At first, Millie was hesitant to make the leap, concerned Adele would let the project drop as soon as she grew tired of it. However, Adele was determined to prove otherwise. In her zeal over a new project and her need to distract herself, she had found a distributor, researched prices, and even designed a sign to hang above the door.

At last, Millie gave in. They signed a rent agreement for the shop and had it open in a matter of weeks.

The shop was a lazy, slow business—but Adele knew how to sell flowers. To husbands, to boyfriends, to fathers, to sons. If women came in the shop, she could flatter them into it, too—but she was best with the men.

At least she was good at something.

She wasn't going to date anymore. That hurt too much. No, it was time to find something better … something more sustainable.

Chapter Eight

Spring 1931
London, England

"You don't sing 'for she's a jolly good fellow,' now, do you?" Dave joked as he set a plate of cake in front of Lola.

Lola swatted in her husband's general direction. "I'm fine with no singing whatsoever if that's all right with you two gentleman."

Troy chuckled. "Fine by me. I know my singing voice isn't quite on pitch."

"It's not on pitch at all." But Lola softened her words with a teasing smile. She even reached across the table to squeeze his hand.

At least she wasn't entirely enamoured with her husband; she seemed capable of paying some attention to Troy still. That was nice. He loved Lola so much, and he had been so afraid she'd ignore him completely. But that didn't seem to be the case.

Not that she still loved him the way she used to.

No, Dave had taken the place of "most important male in her life." But that was as it should be, he supposed.

"What about my voice?" Dave asked, taking a seat by Lola. "Isn't it beautiful?"

"Er, yes. If you like a crow's caw," Lola said, sticking her fork into the cake.

Dave fake-gasped. "I can't believe you just said that, my love! That's hurtful."

"Oh, shush. You know I love you." Her eyes twinkled in that way Troy didn't want them to twinkle at any man, and he growled to himself at the sight of it.

"Yes. I know." Dave leaned over and kissed her. Right on the lips. The man had no shame, kissing his wife like that. It wasn't a long kiss, but it hit Troy right in the gut.

Stupid Dave. Stupid marriage. Stupid kiss.

After the cake was eaten, and Dave and Lola were snuggled up on the couch, Troy excused himself to take a long walk and cool off. It wouldn't do to get mad at Dave again now that the dreaded deed was done. They were family, and he needed to accept Dave—like it or not.

He strolled out on the London street, something he'd not done in ages but rather enjoyed doing. There was a hurried, scurried busyness about London that, though it could be overwhelming at times, also intrigued him. The buzz, the crowds, the various people running about doing who-knows-what, and the cars honking their way by with who-knows-who in them.

He wondered where they were all going in such a

hurry, and he wondered that until he was significantly cooled down and relaxed.

It was all right for Lola to have a husband. He could accept it. It just might take him a bit of time … and a lot of understanding.

It had almost got him to the point where he wished he had his own, female Dave. Obviously, she'd be nothing like Dave, but someone who could be his best friend, who could push him away from his endless drifting in the security of creating and nurturing a family. Without Lola there, he and Harrington had an all right life, for bachelors, but Troy felt the right woman would push him to do things like go to church and not leave his dirty underwear piled in the bathtub.

He strolled onto a pretty little street lined with buildings that had shops on the bottom and apartments above them. It reminded him of the street he'd grown up on, and he looked about, glancing in every shop as he passed it.

As he moved past a flower shop, he looked in the big picture window and stopped dead in his tracks.

Had he caught an angel at work in the mortal realm?

~

"Why don't you go out more often?" Millie asked. She sat behind the counter with Adele in the quiet early afternoon hours as she often did when she had some time off work. "You've stayed home almost every evening of late, and I don't understand it. It's not like you."

Adele set down the bouquet she was making and raised her eyebrows. "*You're* encouraging me to go out? With men? Why, Millie!" She faked a shocked expression.

"I know, I know. It's unlike me." Millie smiled self-consciously. She rose, picked up a small dustpan and hand broom, and swept a variety of leaves, thorns, and other vegetation up. "It's just … I worry for you. I don't want you to be sad. If going out would make you happy …"

"You're sweet, Millie, but I can take care of myself." Adele set the completed bouquet aside, leaned forward on the counter, and played with her wristwatch. "You don't have to worry about my romantic affairs."

Millie sighed. "But I do. I worry about you a lot."

Adele chuckled. "You don't have to."

"I know."

"You see, Millie." Adele struggled for words for a moment then arrived at them. "I'm not really interested in empty flirtations anymore."

Millie considered this for a moment. "I see."

"I've been hurt too many times trying to keep things light. But I'm not made that way. I can and must get attached. But the thing is, I've got to get attached to a man who gets attached to me in return." Adele ran a hand over her eyes. "That's easier said than done, but I'm sure of it."

Millie nodded. "I can respect that. Just … be careful, Adele. It can be so easy to get hurt. I don't feel I need to warn you of that—I know you're very, um, careful where your heart is concerned, or at least you try to be—but … be careful. Take your time. As

Jane Austen said, 'the right man will come at last.'"

She left a few minutes later to go to her 'real job' while Adele remained at the shop. She had quit the department store—it had been a good job, and she'd enjoyed it, but it just wasn't the same as working at the flower shop. This was something really all her own.

Millie, however, liked the safety of her secretary job—and, since she was now in charge of several other typists, it had gotten somewhat lucrative, at least as far as a woman's wages at a government office went.

Adele pulled out her battered copy of *Sense and Sensibility* and began reading, elbows rested on the counter. She found herself almost crying over Elinor and Marianne's troubles. She quickly snatched out her handkerchief, dabbed her eyes, and then stuffed it away to return to her book.

She was just getting to the part where Ferrars returns to Elinor when the bell over the door rang, and she looked up. A tall, somewhat gangly man stood in the doorway. He had strawberry blond hair, just a bit messy, and pale blue eyes. His upper lip sported a neatly-clipped mustache, and he was smiling.

"Hello, there. I imagine you sell flowers?" he said. His accent was English but lower class and with a slight foreign infection.

Adele smothered a laugh. "Yes, sir, we do. What are you looking for?"

"Er, two bouquets. The first is for my sister—it's her birthday, she likes pink roses, and we could add some little white flowers or something; you'll know what to do with that."

Adele nodded. "I can do that easily. And the second bouquet?"

"It's for a special lady. Not sure what she'd like yet, though. If you were to buy yourself a bouquet, what would it look like?"

"What do you know about the lady?" Adele asked.

He grinned self-consciously. "She's quite lovely; that's really about all I know."

Adele laughed. "What kind of lovely?"

He cocked his head to the side, regarding her closely. "Dark beauty. Almost Italian, I'd say."

Adele nodded. "Is this for a formal occasion or …?"

"Um, more of a casual date, I'd say. Dinner, perhaps, but more of a café sort of thing. Perhaps a stroll afterwards in the park. But not too casual. I think she's got some class. Like I said, this is for a lady, not some street girl. Keep that in mind."

"Of course," Adele said. "So we have a very lovely, dark lady for a semi-casual date. And what do you want to communicate with the bouquet? Most women won't think about the 'language of flowers,' but it's wise for us to consider it—just in case. And a few flowers have very obvious meanings. Forget-me-nots, for instance. And most people interpret roses to mean love, though they're also a common flower. Still, they're rather my favorite."

"I think she would know the language of flowers, whatever that is. But that's what I'm not sure about," the man admitted. "I don't want to frighten her off."

"Flowers seldom frighten women," Adele assured him. "I'm assuming this would be a first date?"

"Yes. But I feel strongly that this is it." His voice had a slight crackle about the edges, like he was almost getting emotional about it.

Adele raised her eyebrows. "You're very sure of yourself."

He shook his head. "I may look that way; I'm trembling on the inside. But … yes. As sure as a fellow can be without knowing the lady's mind. I'm only half of the equation, and she makes the final decision."

Adele sighed and turned to collect a catalog. She felt suddenly wistful. Here was a man firm in his path and yet not too overbearing or overconfident. He was definitely a romantic, too, which was always nice. People nowadays didn't believe in romance—at least not romance with happy endings. "So love at first sight?"

"You might call it that."

Smitten. Absolutely smitten. Whoever the girl was, she was a lucky one. It was rarely a man let his feelings get so involved. All the good ones were taken, and the bad ones only made love to good time girls while their wives were nothing but business deals. "Thornless roses, red. How much can you afford?"

"Money isn't an object."

And not too poor. Always nice. "Very well. Here are some of my favorite arrangements."

Once the two bouquets were assembled, the man accepted them both carefully, wrapped up so they would be preserved until the evening, and smiled down at her.

"I forgot I never learned your name," he said.

"Oh. Adele. Adele Collier."

"Adele. Hmm." He seemed to test the name on his tongue. "That's quite pretty. I'm Troy Kee."

She started to extend her hand then laughed when she realized he didn't have the ability to shake, loaded down with flowers as he was. "I'm glad to meet you."

He smiled. "And I am very glad I met you. Actually, I have a question. What are you doing tonight?"

Adele paused, unsure how to respond, then laughed. "Nothing, really."

"Hmm … then I suppose you need somewhere to go for dinner?"

Chapter Nine

Love at first sight wasn't real, was it? That was something made up for fairy tales, for stories that didn't have a grasp of reality.

In reality, a couple had to know each other well to claim such a thing as love. They had to develop the relationship over time—more time than a few milliseconds.

If all this was true, why did he feel like this?

Adele was walking along at his side with her hand in his like she'd known him all his life—and just now it felt like he had.

It was one of those times when he had to pretend to feel less than he did—which was rare for him. Normally he had to be kinder than he felt, warmer than he felt, gentler than he felt. Today he had to hold himself back. He didn't want to scare her, and most of all, he didn't want to leave himself open for the hurt that would inevitably come if he let himself fall too hard too fast.

He'd taken her to dinner and now they were

strolling through the London street. She'd wanted to dance, he could tell, but he wasn't quite comfortable with that. He'd never danced with a woman in his life, and he didn't think starting with a woman one actually liked was a good idea.

"Troy is such an interesting name," she was saying.

"Er, yes. My mother was an interesting person, and she gave both my sister and me unusual names."

"Well, I don't know that Eloise is too unusual," said Adele. "I knew an Eloise where I grew up, and I think Lola is a sweet nickname, too. Was your mother the French one?"

"*Oui.*" He winked. "And yes, I suppose Lola isn't too bad. Just Troy."

She laughed. "I like your name, actually. Roberts and Johns and Joes are all fine and well, but unusual is infinitely more fun."

"What about your mother?" Adele had told him that her father and two brothers had been lost in the war, and had talked about them quite a bit, but she'd barely mentioned Mother except to say that she lived in Kent and didn't get up to London often.

"Oh, she's … conventional." Adele shrugged and squirmed, so he didn't protest when she changed the subject. "Do you enjoy living in France? Is it as romantic as people say?"

"It's lovely, and yes, I think so. I've never been one for romance, but well … I can see that my mind might change." He smiled down at her. Perhaps that was a little much, but he felt it needed to be said. He didn't want her to think that this was just a casual date.

She squeezed his hand but didn't respond to his comments. Yet her expression seemed positive, so perhaps she wasn't entirely opposed to the idea. To him.

They continued talking and walking for hours more.

~

Why did she feel like this?

Adele walked slowly up the steps and arrived at the door of her apartment. She tried the doorknob and pulled out her key to unlock it.

"Could you come in for a second? Millie … I think I'd like to introduce you to Millie."

Troy Kee smiled. "I'd like nothing more."

Adele opened the door and stepped in. Nervously, she moved aside to let her date enter and glanced about the tiny living room. "Millie?"

"In here," Millie called from the bedroom. "You're rather late! Must be one!"

"It's past it. But come out here. I want you to meet someone."

Millie appeared wearing a fuzzy bathrobe over her pajamas. "Oh? And who's this?" Her face lit up with a friendly smile, though her eyes were hesitant behind her glasses. Well they ought to be. Most of Adele's other boyfriends weren't ones Millie could approve of.

But Troy, bless him, was different. He was someone that, well, Adele could take home. It was a new experience, dating a decent man, a man who wasn't carefree and lacking in any proper responsibility or self-discipline.

Troy was a good fellow. And Adele wasn't sure quite what to do with him, or with the bubbling feelings in her chest toward him.

His decency appealed to her, she supposed. She wasn't used to decency appealing to her, but he was so honest and feeling and open that she couldn't help it. She wanted to bury herself in his cleanness and hope it'd rub off on her a bit.

She was starting to feel a bit dirty about the edges, and she wanted to wipe it off a bit. Just give her soul a nice dusting, a bit of sunlight—a spring airing.

"Millie, this is my date, Troy Kee. He … he took me out to dinner …"

"I know, you told me this evening after work." Millie sent Adele a playfully scolding look then approached Troy, hand extended. "I'm Millie Lark, Adele's dearest friend and flatmate. It's a pleasure to make your acquaintance."

Troy smiled. "It's a pleasure to meet you, too, Miss Lark."

"Oh, Millie's fine."

Adele was a bit surprised. Millie usually would respect a "Miss Lark" when it was given to her. However, she wasn't overly shocked. There was something about Troy Kee—and furthermore, something about his way in calling a woman by her last name until she gave him permission to do otherwise—that made one want to give a first name and ask him to use it.

It was the honesty, the cleanliness. He was just so good. Adele tried to think why she was letting herself think this way about a man her mother might actually approve of, but she couldn't come up with an answer.

She liked Troy Kee. She might even be developing a bit of a crush for him. And even her mother's impending approval—if she ever met Troy, that was—couldn't stop her from feeling as she did.

"Thank you, Millie." Another grin from the spit-and-polish man who stood at her side. "Call me Troy, of course."

"I will." She nodded at him then quietly quit the room. Millie was excellent at knowing when an exit would be desired by her best friend.

"Well, then." Adele stood there for a second in silence. She'd let Troy decide their next move. She wasn't sure what good boys did when they dropped a girl off after their first date. From another boyfriend, she'd have given a kiss and a flirtatious remark and perhaps a plan for another date—or, if she felt like it, she might draw back from a request for another date.

But with Troy? Who knew. She was far over her head.

"Thank you for a lovely evening." He said the words rather awkwardly, as if he wasn't sure what to say either. Hat in hand, he inched toward the door. Did that inching mean he respected her enough not to impose or that he wanted to get away? She couldn't decide.

"It was lovely," Adele confirmed. "Can we—I mean do you …?" Her voice trailed off. She knew instinctively that Troy would frown upon her asking for a second date, to see him again, to at least enjoy another wonderful conversation in the future … but she couldn't let him go without a promise. It would drive her mad.

"I hope to see you again soon," Troy said. "I'll … I'll ring up or I'll stop by the shop soon. I want to see you again."

Adele's face broke into a brilliant, spontaneous smile—even though she'd intended to pretend nonchalance and be cool and make him work for it. She couldn't bear that. She was already too attracted to this man. "I want to see you again, too. Soon."

His smile was as bright as hers felt. "Good. Good. I couldn't … I mean, I …" His voice trailed off. "I'll see you soon."

"All right."

He walked away, and she shut the door behind him and sighed, not caring how silly or romantic she was being. She had a gentleman caller coming for her. A handsome gentleman caller—and she wasn't just saying gentleman as a way of describing any male who happened to ask her out.

No, Troy was a true gentleman. Perhaps he wasn't rich or famous or esteemed, but he was a gentleman in all the little ways that mattered, and Adele was oddly fine with this—even thrilled with it.

What on earth was wrong with her?

Adele locked the front door and went into the bedroom where she began removing jewelry, makeup, and clothing.

"Well?" Millie's voice behind her was questioning.

"Well, what?"

"Adele, don't give me that!" Millie giggled. "You're starry-eyed! What happened? Who is he? All I know is that he asked you out today, and you've never seen the man before. Yet look at your face!

You're glowing!"

Adele glanced in the mirror as she set her pearl necklace on the vanity. Millie was telling the truth. Her eyes were sparkling, her lips kept smiling, and she didn't know what was happening to her heart—it kept squeezing and contracting in such an odd way.

Butterflies. She had butterflies. And she'd known the man only since that afternoon! What was wrong with her?

"Adele?" Her best friend would not be brushed off.

"Millie, I think I'm falling in love."

"You've known him all of a few hours!" Millie protested, but she was laughing.

"I know! And that's what makes it so strange. I'm so … I don't know! I don't know what I'm feeling." Adele collapsed onto her bed and stared at the ceiling. "He's so perfect. I don't know how I know it, but we were talking, and everything he said seemed to fit. Fit perfectly with … well, I'd say my idea of a perfect man, but that's not true. He's nothing like men I've imagined falling for!"

"Right down to his mustache!" Millie laughed. "I'd have thought you wouldn't even consider a man with a mustache. I thought you hated the things."

"I do!" Adele could help but chuckle. "I do hate them! But for some reason, with every word he said and every moment we spent together, he was reshaping my idea of a perfect man into what he is. And … I don't know. I couldn't shake the feeling of rightness about it."

"That's nice!" Millie's brow furrowed. "But … Adele, this is all very well and good, but of course you realize that … that … well, one can't fall in love overnight? Even if your feelings get attached that fast, even if you feel that you're falling in love, well, a real relationship develops over time. So if you want something serious, go slowly. Get to know him. Let him get to know you. Don't just fall in love with him —love him, consistently, through your actions and with your spirit and mind as well as your heart and body."

Adele smiled. That was so like Millie. "I'm not about to marry him, Millie. Don't worry about that."

"I know. But getting attached to a man in such a way that reason cannot invade … that's not wise either, even if you don't make it permanent. In fact …" Millie glanced worriedly at Adele then looked away. "In fact, if you let yourself fall in love with him that way, in a way that only concerns how you feel, you know what that leads to."

She nodded. "I don't believe I trust him that much yet." And at the same time, she did. Trusted him more than men she'd known for years. Trusted him with her heart, her soul, her thoughts, her opinions … and trusting him with her body? She could do that. She wanted to.

If she was going to sleep with someone, it ought to be a man who would be responsible, who would be careful of her feelings, and who hadn't already slept with a dozen other women.

Something told her Troy wasn't the type to do that. It would mean something to him, too. It would be special—not just one in a hundred, a fish in a school of equally attractive fish all of whom he could have his way with. She would be unique, remembered, cherished. It wasn't casual to him.

She shook her head. It wasn't something she needed to think about. Who knew where this relationship would go? He must go back to France, his vineyard, his dog, and his friend Harrington soon. She knew that full well. He wouldn't be here long. Surely not long enough to start the kind of relationship Millie spoke of.

So the question was—should Adele leave him be, let a man she thought herself seriously in danger of falling deeply in love with just wander off? Or should she let herself get sucked into the whirlwind and cast her lot now?

Her heart pulled inexplicably toward the latter.

Chapter Ten

"Adele!" She couldn't control the sudden pounding of her heart at the sound of his voice—saying her name, no less—or the sudden rush of blood to her face, but she could control her manner of greeting.

She turned from the door of her flower shop, which she was just leaving to take a lunch break, and smiled as coolly as she could manage. "Why, hello, Troy! I'm glad sooner wasn't later." It was just last night that they'd had their first date, and here he was seeking her out again.

He must really like her. Oh, she hoped so!

"I'm glad, too." He stepped up to her, reached out his hand, then dropped it to his side. His blue eyes shone, and she wondered vaguely if it were for her or if they usually shined like that.

Whatever the reason, gosh, he was handsome.

"Where are you off to?" he asked.

"Lunch break," Adele said. "Would you come with me?" Her words were impulsive, and she almost wished she could call them back, but at the same time

… oh, how she wanted to spend more time with him!

Yes, she had it bad, and she didn't care one bit.

"Actually," Troy said, "I thought you could come with me. You see, Della—"

Her heart crumpled inside her chest. "It's … it's not Della. It's Adele." She couldn't believe he'd forgotten her name! It was a natural mistake, she supposed, but it still hurt. It hurt worse than it should, honestly.

"Oh, I know! I just thought it'd be a rather sweet nickname for you." He smiled. "I like nicknames. Rather give one a sense of … of familiarity." He glanced at her face as if trying to gauge her reaction then continued on. "My name isn't nickname-able, I'm afraid, but I still like giving other people nicknames."

Oh. It was a nickname. Thank goodness! She'd thought she was going to cry for a moment, but a nickname was … lovely. But it shouldn't be *that* nickname. "I like nicknames, too, and I'd be, well, honored to have one—but … it can't be Della."

"Why not?"

Because it's too close to Della-bell, and I don't want to feel like sobbing every time you address me. "Just because. I don't like it."

"But I like it." Troy smiled devilishly. "I think I'll call you that."

She started to protest further, but something in those blue eyes stopped her. He seemed to take such a delight in it—and really, it wasn't "Della-bell" exactly. If he called her that, she couldn't allow it, but … "All right, then. You can call me Della if you like. I suppose it's … it's rather sweet."

"That's exactly what I think!" He grinned. "Now, where was I?"

"Something about you taking me somewhere?"

"Oh, yes!" The grin only seemed to broaden. "Last night when I got home, my sister was up in flames about me leaving her on her birthday and all. And so Lola insisted on meeting the woman that made her brother miss her birthday eve." He smirked. "She wasn't really mad. In fact, I think she's glad I've gotten out a bit. I don't often. But she did want to meet you! So could you come and have lunch with us at their house?"

Something like dread inexplicably filled Adele's chest. She didn't know why. She'd never been nervous about meeting anyone—but the thought of meeting Troy's beloved only sister whom he plainly cared about greatly frightened her. She didn't want to disappoint Troy. She wanted to make a good impression. She wanted … well, she wanted to be the kind of girl a man took home to their family.

But she wasn't that girl. She never would be. Her mother had made that clear, and her lifestyle had made it clearer still.

What does it matter? At least it's not his parents, the sensible side of Adele said. But her heart was much louder, much more insistent, and it said that it did matter. For some odd reason, it did matter, and her mind was unable to convince her heart otherwise.

But she couldn't disappoint Troy no matter how scared she was. So she simply said, "Of course I'll come!"

~

Troy squeezed Adele's arm as they stood outside his sister's flat. He raised his hand as if to knock then realized that was rather silly and opened the door.

"Lola, it's us," he called.

Us was a nice word.

His sister appeared in the living room, a broad smile on her face and a blue checked apron tied about her slim waist. "There you are! I'm so glad you've come." Her eyes were fastened on Adele. "I'm Lola Cole, as I'm sure Troy told you. It's so lovely to meet you—Adele, isn't it?"

"Yes, Adele." Her shining beauty was demure now. "It's nice to meet you, too."

"Why don't you come in? Dave's just in the kitchen—probably sneaking rolls—but I'll make him come and talk to you while I finish."

"Finish what?" Troy sniffed the air. "I hope you haven't gone to a lot of trouble, dear. It's only lunch."

"Well, not a lot of trouble," Lola said somewhat elusively. His sister was actually a half-decent cook—self-taught though she was—and she liked doing fancy things. He wondered what she'd made today.

Dave entered then, shook Adele's hand, and when Lola went back to the kitchen, the three took seats in the living room. To Troy's surprise, Adele sat on the arm of his chair—practically in his lap—rather than taking her own seat like a normal person.

Dave didn't comment on it. He just politely asked Adele a question which she answered evenly. Troy didn't feel obligated to saying anything; she carried the conversation smoothly and naturally.

It would seem this lady knew how to handle a

social situation a great deal better than he did. She was perfectly relaxed, while Troy's heart was pounding, and she didn't seem at all bothered by his silence.

At last Lola called them into the dining room where they partook of some simple but delicious soup.

Adele was perfect throughout the meal. Troy was more than impressed by her. Honestly, this woman was such a joy. Always smiling, always laughing, always gay and carefree. Friendly, vivacious, and kind.

How could he not fall in love with her? It seemed like an impossibility.

He needed to rein this in. He must. There was no other way. Yet the way those brown eyes sparkled, the way she tossed her head, sending her hair sweeping back behind her shoulder, the soft joyfulness of her laugh …

He was lost. There was no way around it.

He rose quickly to clear the dishes when the meal was over. Lola motioned Adele as a guest to sit down, picked up a plate, and jerked her head toward the kitchen. Troy followed her in.

"Troy, I see the look in your eyes and in hers, and I don't like it one bit!" she said.

Troy blinked. "I … what on earth are you talking about, Lola?"

"You know very well what I'm talking about, Troy Kee!" Lola dropped a pile of dishes in the sink with a terrible shattering. "That woman! Who is she? You've known her less than twenty-four hours, and you're acting like you're married, for heaven's sake.

What's wrong with you?"

"Nothing's wrong with me." Troy set the bowls on the counter and stepped back. "She's just … she's a girl I've met. I think I'm falling in love with her."

Lola sighed. "Troy, that's ridiculous. You don't know her! I know you may feel like this is it, but I'll give you the same advice you would give me were you in a more rational state of mind—you have to take your time. Don't wander into any lifelong commitments until you're sure."

Troy sighed. "You're right. I'll be careful."

Yet he knew in his heart that, for the first time in his life, he had told his little sister a lie.

~

Troy walked her back to the shop after lunch. His sister's words weighed heavily on him—but at the same time, he couldn't believe her to be an expert on romance.

This felt unstoppable, unending. He trusted Adele. He'd yet to find anything truly objectionable about her. What was so wrong with that?

Nothing. If he'd found the one—and he was sure he had—why delay? His father had been sure of his mother, after all.

"Della," Troy whispered, ducking his head close to her ear.

"Mm?" She smiled up at him.

"What if I were to say I think I'm falling in love with you?" The words were rushing out of his mouth before he knew what he meant, but they felt right. "Let's just drop everything and spend the day together. I don't have a thing to do, and surely it's not imperative that the shop stay open. Please, Della?"

Her fingers slid into his hand once more and squeezed them. "Yes. Yes, let's … let's just do it. I don't think people are given these sorts of opportunities often in their life, and I don't want to waste it."

"Thank you." He pressed her fingers in hers. "I don't know how long I'll be in England, though I'm thinking I'll have to lengthen my stay if I want to be sane at all. Leaving you would be horrendous." He didn't understand it, but at this point he thought it wasn't worth understanding—just feeling.

She was perfect. She was lovely and kind and sweet and gentle and happy and everything a woman ought to be. Everything his wife ought to be.

Was he moving too fast? Yes, of course, or at least some might interpret it as such. But sometimes moving fast was required. If he knew, why wait? Surely his heart wouldn't fail him in this instance—and he was so very sure.

"And Troy?" Her eyes were twinkling now.

"Yes?"

"I think I'm falling in love with you, too."

Chapter Eleven

It was funny how just about everything Adele suggested doing was something Troy enjoyed as much as she did. Some sort of wondrous luck, she supposed.

She knew he didn't like dancing, so she didn't suggest that, and he seemed to be the quiet sort who wouldn't enjoy a big loud party … but at the same time, she wasn't denying herself for him. She enjoyed the things they were doing just as much.

They explored London together. She saw regular old tourist sites with new eyes. Troy apparently hadn't really seen anything in London since he moved to France at the age of eleven; it was like taking a little country kid for a walk. He was always chattering and pointing, and his enthusiasm passed on to her.

The man wanted to see Westminster Abbey, Big Ben, Buckingham Palace, and the Tower Bridge and art galleries and museums and all the things a typical tourist might go to see. She questioned him on whether or not he was truly a born Londoner, and he simply laughed.

Such boyish joy in seeing old landmarks that one could pass any old day of the week was both amusing and catching.

Feeding the pigeons wasn't something Adele had done since she was a tiny bit of a thing visiting the city with her father or one of her brothers, but she found it was just as fun as she remembered.

"This isn't any real fun, though," Troy said as a few dozen fat, lazy birds flew about them and enjoyed the bread he'd bought from a nearby store.

"Oh? What is?"

"Feeding the crazy seagulls in France." Troy winked. "Those things will dive right at you like they want to take a piece of your eye rather than a bit of bread!"

Adele chuckled. "Now, that sounds like an adventure!"

"It is! And they're funny little things, too. I wish … I wish I could show you."

Adele smirked. "Perhaps you will someday." She hoped so. She wanted to believe for the first time that a man was her future, and she wanted that man and that future to be Troy Kee.

Troy bought a big box of chocolates for them to enjoy. Because of her hips, Adele knew she shouldn't, but she did. He was spending too much and doing so much to impress her, and she couldn't let it go to waste. Even though, she reflected as Troy popped a fifth chocolate into his mouth, he could probably finish off the box himself—and willingly.

They also visited pet store, where Adele cooed over every puppy and kitten, and Troy compared them all negatively to his dog Holt, sending her into fits of giggles.

At last Troy bought a picnic dinner after bribing a restaurant owner something fierce, and they took a cab out of town to find a nice hopefully unowned field to finish off their evening.

The sun dipped gradually toward the horizon, but it was warm, and Adele didn't mind stretching out on the old tablecloth, the grass and earth underneath, and daydreaming. She didn't want the day to end.

Even if Troy had been trying to teach her French all day, and she was failing miserably.

"I tell you, Troy, my mother tried, and my teacher tried, and Millie has tried … I'm hopeless! The pronunciation is beyond me." Adele shook with laughter at another of her hilarious fails, as well as Troy's reaction to it, and dropped her head back on the tablecloth. "It was the worst part of my school day, you know."

"Perhaps you'd have tried harder if you'd known you'd be meeting me." Troy leaned over her and his hand traced down the side of her cheek, his thumb dawdling over her lips.

She drew in a quick breath. "I would have."

As she'd wanted, he shifted closer in response to her low tone of voice. "Perhaps if I'd known there was a woman like you in the world, I would've stayed in England and spent every year since I could walk searching for you."

"Perhaps you would have." Her hand came up, cupped his cheek, touched his mustache disapprovingly, then traced his lips as well. "And I'd be waiting. Well-versed in French."

He grinned. "And I'd be so everlastingly glad to have found you … that I'd pull you into my arms …" He shifted to hold her, brought her body close. "... and I'd kiss you."

"How?" Her voice was nothing but a breath.

His lips were on hers, and she wished it would never end.

~

He truly wished it could go on, but of course it couldn't. Not another second. He told himself that firmly as he pulled back.

"Troy?" Her whispered words, the tone to them, her lazy eyes—stopping wasn't exactly what was on her mind. But he'd be the gentleman and respect her, even if she wasn't in the mood to be respected. "Is something wrong?" Her voice was hurt.

"It's all right. Nothing wrong with … anything." With the kiss or with the beautiful woman before him. "I just think we'd better not go any further."

She propped herself up slightly on her elbows and cocked her head. "I didn't see any problems with what we were doing."

Troy blinked. Oh, she didn't, did she? Well, women were naturally less physically aware, so perhaps to her there wasn't any problems with it—but to him?

What scared him the most was that he'd wanted to disobey God's rules, at least for a moment in time.

"Darling." He tangled his fingers in her brown hair for a moment as he thought. "Darling, if we'd gone on, we'd have been sure to go too far. You know what I mean. I think it's all right for us to have these feelings, but we ought to keep control over them until it's all right for us to—"

"Make love?"

Troy coughed. He hadn't expect that kind of frankness from her. "Yes, well, that."

She smiled. "Troy, I know you think you're doing the honorable thing, and under most circumstances you would be! I appreciate it when men respect that. And I've never let myself go any further than a few kisses with a man before."

She seemed embarrassed to admit it which confused Troy. Wasn't that something every woman could claim? Some, he thought, hadn't even gone as far as a few kisses. If they were kisses like he'd just given her, he didn't like to think that Adele had done that with another man.

It didn't seem right to just peddle affection around from one person to another. It ought to be more special to kiss someone. Yet he supposed he couldn't judge Adele for it.

"That's … that's good." How else did one respond to that sort of statement?

"But … but …" She blushed. "Troy, you're different. You're honorable and sweet, and I know … I know you'll take care of me. You'd be gentle and considerate. So, no. I don't think we need to stop."

Troy stared at her. His mind must not be feeding him the correct information from his ears.

Her hand slid over his. "Troy? I … I guess I'm offering myself to you. I know you're a good man. I trust you. I'm not afraid. Those are the main things, after all, aren't they?" She leaned toward him, but

Troy jumped back.

"Those aren't the main things at all." He stood quickly and paced a few steps away from her. "Della, have you taken leave of your senses? The main things are a marriage license and a ring on your finger and a honeymoon. The main things are us pledging our lives to each other. It has nothing to do with how either of us feel or if we're attracted to each other—I mean, it does, but it doesn't."

He knew he was spilling out whatever words came to mind, but they made more sense than Adele's had, which was something.

~

Confused and a bit frightened, Adele sat up and stared at the man she cared for more than anything else in the world—the man she'd just offered herself to and been rejected by.

She didn't understand one bit. They were as good as committed, and she was willing that marriage should come sometime down the line—but why should it come before they were absolutely sure? And how could they be absolutely sure if they didn't experiment a little?

It wasn't just that, though. It was also a commitment she wanted to make—he was someone she could trust. Her inexperience wouldn't be exploited; he wouldn't hurt her; she wouldn't be left to pick up any broken pieces by herself. He was a better sort than every other man she'd ever dated.

But as Troy stood there staring at her, something uneasy filled her chest. In his eyes, she could see a trace of something she knew well—disgust. It was heavily mixed with worry, fear, frustration, and confusion, but it was there, buried beneath all the other emotions.

Only bad women offered themselves to men like that. Good girls waited until the wedding night. That was how it was supposed to be. And, because Troy was a traditional and honorable, he believed that, too.

She'd forgotten for a moment, when she wanted him, that even her perfect man couldn't be spotless. He was stained with morals that did no one a bit of good.

She stood as well. "I'm so sorry, Troy." She held a hand out to him then dropped it to the side, looked at her feet, feigned embarrassment. "I didn't … I wasn't thinking. I was caught up in the moment, and I only wanted to be with you. I forgot. Of course. How stupid of me."

She glanced up. His eyes had gentled; the disgust was gone, most of the fear and frustration, and all but the barest traces of worry and confusion. He even smiled with half of his mouth in an adorable way.

"That's all right. We all get carried away, I'm sure. I almost did."

"Thank you. Truly, do you forgive me?" Best to rub it in as much as she could. She wanted this to be believable. She couldn't lose him. Not when he actually cared about her. Not when he actually listened. Not when he was so sweet and good.

"Of course I do. Let's pretend it never happened. I'm rather good at forgetting things." He stepped forward and took her hands. A quick brotherly peck to the forehead, though, and he stepped back again.

"We've got to be good, all right? That's what God would want. Let's get our picnic cleaned up, and I'll take you home."

Adele blinked. Oh, so he really was religious. Well, best to get that illusion out of the way now, at least. "I've never really understood Christianity." She laughed to herself. "Or I suppose, rather, it's never understood me."

Troy's eyes swung back to her face. "What do you mean?"

"Oh, I've just never gotten along well with religion, I suppose." She shrugged, not sure how to explain it. "You see, my mother was a strong Christian, but she … she rather hated me."

A soft light chased away another hint of worry in those blue eyes. "Oh! I see. Well, I'm terribly sorry about that." He took her hand and squeezed it. "Thankfully, God heals all, right?"

Adele cocked her head, not sure what that had to do with it. "Well, I've never known Him to, but I don't really think about those things. God's not really a part of my life."

~

This must be just what it feels like to have a load of bricks dumped unceremoniously on your chest.

"What do you mean by that?" Troy asked weakly.

"Oh, I …" She looked away, guilt tracing her features. "I don't know. I've never been accepted into church—especially recently—because I … I give the appearance of evil, given the crowds I run with. My mother always said I was a demon." The tightness around this last word sounded as if she believed it.

He coughed. "You're not a demon—demons are spirits, and you're a human. You could be demon-possessed, but I'm reasonably sure there'd be a few more warning signs."

Adele blinked then laughed wryly. "That's comforting."

"I'm serious, though, Della." He reached a hand out to her. Her fingers slid into his. "You're just *you*. You're not anything particularly evil. I've only known you a short time, but in that time, you've proven yourself to be a wonderful, sweet, kind, lovely woman, and I can't believe anyone would tell you there was a thing demonic about you."

"I don't think she meant it in the sense of actual demons."

"Even so, that's a terrible thing to say to anyone." He drew her close. "You're capable of making your own decisions as to which master you serve. Not—" He hesitated. "Well, I have no idea what it's like for demons, but I believe it's best not to think on them at all."

"Speak of the devil and all?" There was a smirk playing about those pretty lips that he didn't particularly like.

"Yes, exactly." He forced his voice to be gentle but firm. "You don't want to internalize on darkness. It's not good for you. But what I mean is that you can and should be good no matter how mean-spirited people say you are. You can only serve one master—so be careful that it's God. He's the hero in this fairytale."

A slow nod from the woman who stood before

him. “I see. That … that makes sense. I suppose I never thought I was evil, but it’s … it’s nice to hear it confirmed that I’m not. It can be difficult to believe when everyone tells you otherwise. I’ve been rejected so many times—my mother, church ladies …”

Her voice trailed off. He wasn’t sure if it was because of the magnitude of the people who thought her beyond salvation or because she’d run out.

“So you’re not a Christian?” He might as well have the facts straight now.

“No. I’m not.”

Another pain to his heart. He wanted so badly to marry her. He wasn’t even sure why he wanted it so badly, but he did.

But he couldn’t marry a non-Christian. It was against all the rules he’d learned as a young man. He knew that very well. However, it was so hard to resist when she ticked every other box on his list.

He stared at her eyes, took in big brown eyes pleading with him not to leave, skin just a bit darker than the average English rose and tinged with pink, soft curly mahogany locks … how could he not be with her? He loved her. It was insane to leave a woman he loved.

He could help her along. Show her the good side of Christianity. And, in time, she would—she must—come to love God. There was no way around it. Exposure to the truth would bring it on, and in no time she would be utterly perfect in every way.

He loved her too much to give her up, so she must become a Christian. It was the only way.

“Troy.” Her words were very soft but they trembled. “Troy, does this change things between us?

I … I couldn't bear if it does. I love you so much. You must know that I do. You're so good; why would I not love you?"

You're so good. Only because of God in him. Already she was drawn to the light. There was hope.

"Troy, please don't leave me over this. I … I couldn't bear to be rejected by you over religion. It would break my heart. Let's not let something so trivial come between us. I need to be with you."

He winced at the word 'trivial,' but he understood the feeling. That this couldn't be the end. That he had to make this go on—somehow.

"It's all right. I'm not that kind of Christian." *Not the kind who rejects sinners. Not the kind who abandons a lost soul and hopes all goes well.*

Not the kind of man who would give up all for his God, including the woman he loved.

Not the kind of man who obeyed God's Word when it was inconvenient.

Not the kind of man who put aside his own feelings and followed, even when it was hard, even when it broke him.

No, he was not that kind of man. He knew it even as he pulled her close, pressed a kiss to her hair, let her cuddle into him, and whispered soft endearments.

He'd gone too far to turn back now.

Chapter Twelve

Two Weeks Later

Adele stood before the judge and signed a binding contract. Said words that she didn't know she believed about clinging and cleaving and loving him for the rest of her life. Commitments that were beyond her to promise.

His eyes were solemn but sparkling, and she knew he was happy. Glad they'd made this decision.

She wasn't so sure. She'd said "yes" and then "I do," but how could anyone be sure of these things? This was the rest of her life. *What if*s fluttered about her mind.

What if he stopped loving her some day?

What if she stopped loving him?

What if there were children—Heaven forbid it? She couldn't be a mother. She knew that for a certainty. She could barely manage herself.

What if something—anything—went wrong?

They were pronounced man and wife.

Millie pressed her close and congratulated her, but her heart wasn't in it. Adele would wager that Millie had more doubts than she did. Not to mention she'd been reluctant to close down the flower shop, even though Adele was planning on renting it out and using the money to pay her half of the apartment she'd shared with Millie. Meanwhile, the rest of Uncle Caleb's money sat safely in a bank. She didn't want to share that particular account with Troy until she had a good reason to—it was hers, after all—so for now, it was just accumulating interest.

Lola hugged her—Adele was fast learning that Lola was a hugger—and Dave shook her hand. Adele followed Troy out of the courthouse and into a cab.

There was no white dress. She wore one of her better frocks, but it wasn't a wedding dress.

She supposed Millie, Lola, and Dave counted as "family and friends," but it wasn't the huge crowd childhood dreams had conjured.

There was no cheering or thrown rice. No flowers. She'd known for a long time that her father wouldn't walk her down the aisle, but at least she'd imagined a church and a clergyman.

Yet she had Troy, and he seemed to be as much in love with her as a man could be.

When they got to the hotel, she rang he rmother. "Mother, I'm married."

"So now you've done it. That's permanent," Mother said. It was impossible not to feel the heartbreak in her tone. Mother sounded like she might cry. "You can't get out of that commitment, Adele. I hope you know that."

"I know it." Much as it scared her, she was aware of it. At least she wasn't in denial any longer; it wasn't all some picnic that she could frolic out of at any time. She was good and stuck.

Already she felt the ropes begin to chafe.

"It's a pity, really," Mother said. "You never listen to me. I might have been able to advise you out of this hasty marriage, but of course you're not keeping in contact, so it's not as if I knew …" Her words spoke heavily of *my only daughter didn't invite me to her wedding and now I'm jolly well not going to let her forget it,* which Adele supposed was fair enough.

She had been hasty. Too hasty to think. Too hasty to let anyone talk her out of it. But she loved Troy. Wasn't that enough?

"Listen, Mother. I'm calling from a hotel, so I'm going to go now. This is my wedding night, and I don't want you ruining it. Troy and I want to come see you before we leave for France."

"Oh, is that his name?"

"Yes, Troy Kee. He's an Englishman who currently resides on the Riviera. He owns a vineyard, has a sister who is married and lives in London, and a dog named Holt. If you'll let us visit, we'll stop by and talk for a bit and tell you all the rest."

Adele didn't want to, but Troy had insisted. He didn't think it was fair for Adele to leave her mother entirely out of things. He'd already been hesitant about not inviting Mother to the wedding.

Besides, her mother wouldn't have understood the need for a civil ceremony. Even Troy had hesitated, but he'd gone along with practically everything so far.

She might as well give him this small concession—he would meet her mother and probably, knowing Troy, apologize for the fact that she hadn't been invited to watch a judge pronounce them married.

"Yes. You may come." Mother's voice was cold. "Don't expect me to condone this, though. Who knows what immoral rake you've married."

"He's actually rather nice, Mother. Why don't you wait to meet him until you pass judgement?" Adele was surprised at how tired her own voice sounded.

"I know the type of men you run with, Adele."

Mother really didn't, but Adele didn't feel like arguing. "I've got to go now, Mother. We'll drop by Monday next."

"Hmph. Well, all right then. What time?"

"Around tea."

"Fine." The receiver on the other end was slammed down with a clink. Adele set the hotel phone down.

~

"Why do I sense you're more nervous than I am?" Troy asked as he slid out of the cab they'd taken from London to Northern Kent.

Adele shrugged and accepted his help to stand. Her mother had a way of ruining all her dreams, and that was sure to include her dream of having a decent relationship with the man she loved.

Mother would no doubt nitpick at Troy and make him infinitely less attractive in her clouded eyes. And poor Troy didn't deserve it.

Adele hated to think that she'd have to hear a barrage against him. It was bad enough when it was herself—but the man she loved? He was so perfect and kind and good. This was going to be a difficult and upsetting conversation.

They walked up the path to the austere house, and Troy knocked on the door. Adele wouldn't. She wasn't going to make Troy's berating happen any faster than it had to. They stood outside for several long moments before Mother opened the door. She didn't say a word—simply stepped aside and gestured in.

Troy and Adele walked into the formal parlor and took a seat. It had been years since Adele had seen her mother, been in this house, and she felt uncomfortable now in the rooms she'd grown up in. It was a strange feeling, and she wasn't quite sure what to think of it.

"So you're Troy Kee," Mother said. It was a statement, not a question.

Troy nodded. "I am, Mrs. Collier. It's a pleasure to meet you. I've been looking forward to it."

Adele's mother flicked her eyes between the two of them. "Have you now?"

Troy grinned, his most charming one. It came from the depths of his heart right to his face and drew the watcher in. "Indeed, I have! Why shouldn't I look forward to meet you? You're family now. I rather miss having family—all I've got now is Lola."

"Your sister?"

"Yes, Mrs. Collier." He cocked his head. "My father was lost in France and my mother to the

Spanish flu, so it's Lola and me alone. Only Lola's married now, so it's just been me." He turned his eyes to Adele. "That's why I was so glad to meet your daughter. She's given me a new life, honestly."

Mother's eyes seemed to soften a bit as Troy spoke. Adele didn't think it was possible, but Troy had seemed to have had that affect on people. Still, it was entirely unprecedented in Mother's case. It was ridiculous that even Troy could crack through her mother's hard shell.

Yet he seemed to be doing just that.

"I truly am sorry that we were so hasty, though."

Adele glanced sharply at her husband. *What on earth?*

"Oh?" Mother's curiosity was obvious piqued.

"I wish we'd taken the time to have a proper wedding, with you there," Troy said smoothly. "It's just, well, loving Della as I did—and perhaps, a bit, because I don't really care for big weddings—I didn't want to wait. That was selfish of me, I know." He dropped his eyes and clenched his trouser legs in his fists.

Adele had to smother a laugh. Her husband was a champion actor. He'd almost had her convinced of his penitence for a moment there. But she could see through it now. Her mother, however? Mother was eating out of Troy's hand.

"Of course I can understand young people wanting to be together," she said.

Adele thought for a moment that she was going to choke on her own tongue. It was like she was living out some odd, opposites-only dream where her mother was the type of person who understood "young people." She pinched herself and felt the pain but still didn't believe it could be true.

She felt quite off-balance indeed!

Mother and Troy fell to chatting about this and that, perfectly at ease with each other. At last Mother rose.

"I'll get us some tea," she said.

Troy instantly stood. "I could help you, Mrs. Collier. Is there a tray you need carried?"

"No, Troy, that's quite all right. You're a guest; we don't let guests do things." She glanced at her daughter. "But I do want Adele to come with me." She turned and left the room.

Adele glared at her husband, who she was sure had triggered the sudden desire for company in Mother's veins, and followed her mother to the kitchen.

"He's a nice young man, Adele," Mother said when Adele entered the room. "I judged you wrongly there. What you've done to convince him that you're worth a second glance is beyond me—but he's nice."

Adele wasn't sure whether to laugh or cry. She wasn't worth a second glance—but it took all of ten minutes for Troy to win her mother over? The world was a cruel and unfair place. But for once she remained silent. She had nothing to say which could contradict her mother's claim.

Chapter Thirteen

Summer 1931
Paris, France

"While we're here, I have some shopping to do," Adele said. She was practically skipping, had been ever since they'd arrived in Paris. Troy was thrilled that she was enjoying France so much. Apparently visiting the City of Lights was a bit of a childhood dream—but he supposed it was for many little girls. At least, so he'd heard.

"Shopping?" Troy chuckled. "On your husband's banknote, I've no doubt."

"Oh, yes." Adele grinned at him, and he knew he wouldn't protest it one bit. He was currently willing to lose all his money, all his property, even himself to make her happy. And what was wrong with that? She was his bride. He ought to spoil her a little.

"What do you have in mind?"

"Oh, a new gown." She held the edge of her skirt in one hand as swished it back and forth. "Jewelry, maybe."

"Sounds expensive."

"Well, it is Paris, Troy. We don't want to waste it." She clung to his arm, leaned her head against him for a second as they walked, and he knew that absolutely no wasting of Paris would be happening.

Hopefully his bank account wouldn't groan too heavily under the pressure of thoroughly enjoying Paris.

"If it makes you happy," he said softly.

"It does." Another little skip from her, and she dragged him across a crowded street full of honking cars and jostling crowds to visit a little shop filled with pastries whose prices made him wince—though of course he couldn't let his wife see that. It was good to see her eat; sometimes it could be somewhat of a trial to get her to do so.

Some time later in the day, they sat in front of a little cafe watching the cars go by. Adele turned to him.

"Do you have a car?"

"No."

"Why not?"

"The town where we'll live is very small. You can walk to the train station, to the shops … just about anywhere. There's no need for a car." Also, cars were incredibly expensive to buy and maintain. His budget couldn't afford it. But he wouldn't tell her that. No, Adele didn't need to worry about financials.

"Oh, Troy!" Adele was laughing at him, her eyes sparkling, her head thrown back. "Troy, Troy, Troy! It's not about whether or not you *need* a car. Surely you want one?"

Troy swallowed. Trinkets and clothing and

bonbons were one thing—but cars another. "It's an expense that we don't need," he admitted.

"But surely we can afford it?" Adele cocked her head. "So many people have cars. I've always wanted one."

She's always wanted one. Troy's insides clenched. Then she'd best have one. "Well, that rather changes things." He grinned. "What color should we get?" He gestured toward the traffic in the street.

"Silver." Adele's voice was firm. She'd definitely been thinking about this before—probably only waiting for the right moment to bring it up.

Still, he nodded. "Silver it is, Della."

~

They bought the car a few towns over and drove it home to the vineyard. Adele was thrilled, absolutely bouncing in her seat. Troy was trying to pretend he hadn't been cheated out of a large percentage of last year's profits.

"Do you think Harrington will like me?" She wasn't insecure, really; the question came from idle curiosity more than anything. That was what he loved about her. She was always so confident about everything. Not afraid about whether or not people thought badly of her.

"Oh, I don't know. Harrington doesn't outwardly show it if he likes anyone." Troy shrugged and steered the car back onto the right side of the street. He might know how to drive, but he tended to get distracted, and the car tended to wander off the street or into the other lane.

"But inwardly?"

"Inwardly, I think he'll love you. Or at least in time. You just can't give up on him." Troy winked at her before quickly returning his eyes to the road. He'd learned a few miles into the drive that looking at Adele, no matter how much he wanted to, was a bad idea if he wanted them both to live until they arrived home.

At last they drove up the broad drive and parked in front of the misshapen house. For the first time in a long time, Troy was legitimately ashamed of his home.

What if Adele didn't think it was as charming as he did? What if she found it old-fashioned and odd? What if she didn't want to live there? All the *what if*s ran through his mind in circles.

"Well?"

"How lovely!" She jumped out of the car. "There must be some marvelous views around here, aren't there?"

Troy shut off the car and stepped out himself. "Y-yes. There are quite a few, I'd say."

"How wonderful." She turned in a full circle, beaming. "Yes, I think I'll like it here."

He thought his chest was about to cave in with relief, but it didn't. He staggered up the steps after her.

She reached for the doorknob.

"Adele, be careful, won't you? There's—"

The door opened, and a mass of yellow tackled Adele to the ground.

"Holt."

Troy jogged up the steps and grabbed his dog by

the collar. Holt whipped around and tried to tackle Troy next. He didn't quite manage it, though. He was a big dog, but his paws only reached Troy's chest; still, with a bit of jumping, he thoroughly covered Troy's face in kisses and dog drool.

At last he managed to get the dog sitting properly in front of him, though Holt was still wriggling with joy. Troy couldn't help but smile. "Missed me, didn't you?"

Then he remembered and turned to help Adele dust off her new suit. "I'm terribly sorry about that, Della. He just gets in a bit of a mood, and he can't be stopped. He's glad to see me, is all; he's not usually so enthusiastic."

That was a bit of a lie—Holt was often enthusiastic, but then Troy claimed he was still a puppy at a year old. It was to be expected. Soon he'd settle down. Perhaps.

Adele was frustrated, he could tell, but she was trying to make a cheerful face about it, at least. "It's fine. I don't mind," she said. "Don't worry about it. I … I just didn't realize Holt was so big."

Considering the fact that he had a tendency of referring to Holt as a puppy, that wasn't surprising. She'd probably been imagining a sweet little thing, all rolly polly and tiny and mischievous.

Well, Holt was mischievous; he just wasn't tiny or rolly polly. But Troy did love his dog. He hoped Adele would come to love Holt, too.

"Yes, well, he's going to get bigger, too." Troy rubbed the back of his head. "Um, why don't I show you the bathroom so you can clean up a bit?"

He'd soon learned that whenever Adele got dirt on her or anything of the sort, she wanted to wash up. He'd never known a woman so meticulous about her appearance. Lola wasn't like that, at least, and he didn't remember that his mother had been.

He took Adele in, leaving Holt outside to think about his crimes, showed her the bathroom, and collected their suitcases from the car. Adele had a big trunk a friend had loaned her which had been shipped over ahead of time.

Which Harrington had left lying in the middle of the hall.

That was Harrington, all right. Always going above and beyond the call of duty for his friends.

After seeing that the suitcases were stored safely away, Troy went to Harrington's little bedchamber behind the living room. Harrington was sitting in his armchair reading what appeared to be a Russian novel, though Troy couldn't be sure.

"Hmph," said Harrington.

Troy had known that was coming, and he deserved it. Well, best get this conversation over.

He cleared his throat. "Harrington, I'm sorry I didn't invite you to my wedding. It was also rather sudden, you see. I didn't know it was happening myself until a few days before …"

"Um-humph," said Harrington.

"Would you come out and meet my wife? I'm sure you'll like her."

"Hmm-hmph," said Harrington.

"Please, Harrington? I promise you I won't leave you out of any major life decisions from now on."

At last Harrington put down his book. "Goodness knows I'm not your father. You can do what you like. You don't need my permission. Apparently"—humph-hmph—"you don't even need my presence!"

"Harrington, I said I'm sorry. And I am. Terribly. I promise you it won't happen again." He couldn't help smirking a bit.

Even Harrington had to lighten up a bit at that. "Good."

At last his friend stood and followed Troy into the hall. Adele was waiting there. She immediately stepped toward Harrington, beaming, hand extended.

"Hello, I'm Adele."

Harrington didn't shake her hand. He just regarded Adele rather skeptically, probably not sure if he was going to kick her out or not. Well, Harrington could think whatever he wanted to think about Adele, but this was Troy's home, too, and his wife was most decidedly staying in it.

Adele's hand dropped to her side. "How have you been?"

"Well enough. Bored."

"Sorry about that. Hopefully it'll be a bit better now that Troy and I are here to keep you company." Adele slipped her arm through Troy's. "Well, let's get settled in and then we can eat."

Troy nodded. "Yes, let's do that." He was honestly impressed with Adele. She was unperturbed by Harrington's rudeness. That was his wife. He squeezed her hand as they walked up the stairs.

She grinned up at him. "You know, I think I like him. He's an interesting character, and I don't mind his grumpiness. I'm sure he'll warm up to me soon, anyway."

Troy didn't know about that—Harrington wasn't exactly the friendly sort—but he pulled her close and told her he was sure of it, too.

~

"Where are you taking me?" Adele glared at her husband as he dragged her through the rows of grapes. It was a hot day, and she didn't feel like a run. "Honestly, Troy! How much further is it?"

"Not far. Trust me, it's worth it." He grinned back at her, eyes shining, and she couldn't help but smile in return.

At last they arrived at the end of the row and came to a spot with a brilliant view of the Mediterranean, sparkling blue below them.

"Oh," Adele exhaled. "Troy, how beautiful!"

"Come and sit." He gestured to a large flat rock. "I like to come out here and think sometimes. Usually by myself." Something about his tone said that it wasn't a place he shared with many, and she felt honored.

Adele took a seat on the rock. "I love it."

He was beaming. "Do you really?"

"I do." A breeze blew up from the sea and cooled her face. She sighed. "I can see why you'd want to come out here. It's perfect. Definitely something to share."

"I agree." He placed kisses on her cheek, her nose, then her lips. "You know who else is perfect?"

Adele smiled. "I have an idea, but it's not me." She took his hand. "You know I love you, don't you?

I know I don't say it often." *It's a scary thing to say. It leaves me open for so much hurt. I don't know that you'll always love me ... no one else has.*

"Oh, I think you say it often enough." He put an arm around her shoulders and gave her a somewhat awkward but warm hug. "Besides, I know."

"You do?"

"You agreed to marry me, didn't you?" He gave her a quick squeeze. "I think that's rather a sign of love."

"A sign? It should be a confirmation." She snuggled her head into his shoulder. It was really too hot to cuddle, though, and she leaned back after a moment.

There was a long moment of silence, then Troy spoke. "I love you, too. Very much. You're my favorite person. And I feel … I feel very blessed to have you here with me."

Adele also felt blessed, though that wasn't exactly how she would have chosen to express it. "You're my favorite person, too."

Chapter Fourteen

"What?" The word burst from her lips even before her mind and heart could echo the same sentiment.

"You're pregnant, *Madame* Kee."

"But …" She wanted to say, *I can't be*—but the only reason she couldn't was because she didn't want to be. There was no denying it on any logical grounds. "But I hadn't planned on it," she ended feebly.

The French doctor chuckled softly. "That is often the case, *madame*. But surely you suspected …?"

She'd wondered, for a millisecond in time, but told herself she'd been too careful, that it had to be something else. It was times like these when being diagnosed with cancer or mad cow disease looked bright.

"I thought I must be ill or … or something. I didn't know. I thought I'd taken precautions."

"But you're married, *oui*? Surely it doesn't matter. Or will *Monsieur* Kee mind?"

Troy? She wasn't sure how he'd react. She'd never seen him around a child, and they'd not discussed it. He'd raised a dog by hand, though, which was more mothering than she had ever done. "I don't think so. At least, not once he gets used to it."

"Then everything is *très bon*?" The doctor cocked his head and twisted his greased mustache tips in his fingers.

His, Adele thought idly, *is a lot worse than Troy's. Small mercies.*

"*Bon* may be a bit … much," she said at last. "But thank you. Er, *merci*."

"*C'est bon.* Don't worry. I'm sure it's all right. *Enfant* is—how do you say?—blessing!"

Adele sighed and rose from the seat. "That's what I'm told." But she'd seen no real proof of it. Every child she'd ever met was screaming or kicking or running about and doing what it wasn't supposed to be. She'd never even liked children when she was one—and now she, an adult woman, was required to play nanny for the next eighteen years when she had a life to be lived?

No, thank you. Not her. Not Adele.

Could the doctor be wrong? Perhaps he could be. Perhaps she really did have an illness of some sort. It was to be hoped for, at least.

Her feet dragged as she left the office. Troy had taught her to drive over the past month, and, miracle of miracles, let her take the car into town for the appointment. She'd been vague, called it a checkup so he wouldn't make a fuss, drive her in, and smother her for three to six months while she recovered from what she'd hoped had been a bit of exhaustion combined with bad eating and sleeping habits.

Now he'll be smothering me for the next seven or

eight months—and no doubt afterward, too. Très bon, *indeed.*

But I can't be pregnant! I can't be. I wasn't made for motherhood. I can't do this. She slid behind the steering wheel of the shiny silver car and dropped her head forward into her hands.

Then she straightened, dashed a hand over her eyes, and shook herself like a good English girl. *It's all right. I just need to get home and think about this a bit. No use worrying about it now. Let's just get home, talk to Troy, and see what he says.*

~

Troy was outside before she had a chance to turn off the engine; he must have been waiting for her.

"Della! How'd it go?" He opened her car door and stood there, eyes worried.

Of course he was worried. Even though she'd told him it was just a checkup, nothing more, he was still worried. What right did he have to worry and fuss over her so? She was a grown woman. She could take care of herself.

It's his fault, you know. The ugly words crept into her heart before she could stop them. *You wouldn't be pregnant if it weren't for him.*

Well, it does take two ...

Yes, but which of you doesn't want this? Not him. It doesn't matter to him. He doesn't have to carry a human being in his body, bring it into the world, and do the lion's share of the raising. He can run off and leave you to do all the heavy lifting, just like your father. Men aren't involved. They don't have to be.

It's Troy's fault.

"Fine." She hadn't known that one word could sound so harsh until that moment.

Troy blinked and stepped back. "All right, then. How'd it really go?"

Adele stepped out of the car, ignored Troy's offered hand, and marched up the front steps of the house.

"Er, Della?" She could hear his footsteps behind her, but she didn't look back. "Please tell me you're not seriously ill, or I'll go mad."

"Why, would it matter to you?" That sounded irrational even as she said it, but she was rather in an irrational mood. This hadn't been her day.

"Yes, a little." His hand caught her arm in the front hall. "Come on, now. Out with it. Can't be anything we can't get through together, right?"

He wanted her to look him in the eyes and tell him, go to his arms and cry until it was all better. However, crying wasn't going to help this one bit. As far as Adele knew, crying was not an acceptable cure for pregnancy.

"Don't you touch me." She jerked back from him. "It's all your fault."

"What, did you catch the cold I had last week?" He'd put on a cheerful expression, an easy smile, but she could see fear in his eyes. So she'd scared him. Good. He needed to be scared. It made her feel better in an odd way.

"No. Not a cold, *Monsieur* Kee. It's going to last a bit longer than that, and it's going to be a bit more painful, and it's never going to go away. I just … I hope you're satisfied!"

Troy reached for her again then dropped his arms to his sides. "Della, honestly, I cannot think of a thing that, if it's going to cause you this much stress, would satisfy me. Come on. Let's talk. What did the doctor say?"

"I'm pregnant."

There were a few seconds when he just stared at her as if the words were unfamiliar to him. "Pregnant?"

"Yes."

"With … a baby?"

"No, a pumpkin."

"My baby?"

"No, Holt's! For heaven's sake, Troy, can you stop gaping like a goldfish and—"

She was in his arms being smothered against his shoulder and whispered endearments to and told she was loved, cherished, and protected. That she didn't have to worry about a thing.

"Troy!" She pushed him away. "Didn't you hear me?"

"Of course I heard you! And I'm so glad, Della. Oh, gosh. This is incredible. Can we tell people? I mean—gosh, I mean, not everyone, but Lola and … do you want to tell your mother? I'm not sure if you want to tell your mother. I also want to tell *Madame* Bernard because she was teasing me just the other week … but I suppose you wait a few months to tell people? Until, you know, you can tell a bit better? How does that work exactly? Sorry, but I've never had a baby before."

"Troy!" But was she surprised, really? It was just like him to have his priorities mixed up. Thinking about telling people about the baby when here she was, pregnant, and only twenty-two! That wasn't nearly old enough to be a mother. She wasn't sure thirty-two was old enough to be a mother.

"What? Can you tell people?" He reached for her again, like he thought she wanted to be held after all that. "Or not? I don't care. I'm glad I know! I think this is just fantastic." He was beaming. "Oh, what about Harrington?"

Adele threw her hands up. "What about him?"

"I mean, I don't think I can live with the man and not tell him! Besides, on occasion Harrington can be insightful, so if we want to hush it up a few weeks—" He paused and cocked his head. "Why are you frowning?"

"Because you're not listening to me!"

"Of course I'm listening." Another attempted hug which she barely managed to ward off.

"No, you're not." Adele stamped her foot. "Troy Kee, I don't want your baby! I don't want to carry it and give birth to it and raise it. I don't want anything to do with it. Why would I? Are you insane? Do you even know what this is going to require of me? Why, I'm not even going to have it until … until next June or something like that. And babies are messy and smelly and ugly and noisy … ugh!" She shook her head. She felt sick, hated that she felt sick, and hated that Troy was staring at her like she'd lost her mind.

"You don't know, Troy! You're not going to have to do this. You've contributed your tiny part to the making of this child, and you're done, and that's it. That's all a man does, and then he sits back and watches the woman struggle through it! This is your fault, Troy; this is all your fault. I didn't want this. I never wanted this!

"You won't be here for it. You do know that, don't you? You may think you'll be some fantastic father who'll, I don't know, teach your son to shoot or ward off scary suitors from your daughter, but in reality, being a father means *nothing*." Her arms dropped her sides, and her chest heaved. She still couldn't believe this was happening.

"My father meant everything to me," Troy said quietly. "He's the reason I am the man I grew up to be. And he died when I was eleven. I can only imagine how grand it would have been to have him for the rest of my boyhood."

"Oh, shut up. I've seen what men do. They make you think you can rely on them, and then they're not there, and there's your mother—and she's not a good mother, and you feel unloved, and your only option is to get away—oh, I don't need to explain this to you. You can't understand."

"Della, this isn't about us, is it?" He took a step forward. "You don't have to repeat a pattern, you realize? You can … you can be a much better mother than yours was—and I can be a better father. I promise I can. I'm going to be. I know it."

"It's not about my parents, Troy." Adele waved this notion off with a flick of her hand. "It's just a generalization."

"Okay. Let's be the exception to the rule."

"Troy, no. I just … no. I don't want this baby." Adele ran a hand over her eyes. "I wish … I wish this had all never happened."

Adele almost thought Troy's eyes were damp. "I

… I always thought … well, don't you want to start a family with me? Isn't that rather what new couples are supposed to do? Start a family?"

"No, of course not! I didn't marry you to carry on some archaic tradition. Can't you understand that I don't want to have children?"

He flinched. "I'm sorry you feel that way, but we haven't a choice," he said, his voice raising for the first time. "We're going to have a baby, Della. There's no way around it anymore. It's not like you can turn back; it's not like there's anything I can do to stop this. So stop being such a selfish—"

With the fury in her chest turning her vision black, she stepped forward and slapped him across the cheek. "Don't you dare talk to me like that! Don't you dare." She stepped back quickly, panting, and caught herself against the stairwell.

"Della!" His eyes went from shocked to concerned, and he reached for her. "Should you sit down?"

She pushed him away. "Leave me be! I don't want to sit down." A cruel feeling entered her chest, and she smiled. "Maybe if I keep active I'll miscarry."

Troy's jaw clenched and his eyes narrowed. "Adele Kee, you will not take the life of my child because you are too selfish to bring him or her into the world. Don't even talk about it. It just shows what an unfeeling, cruel woman you are, and it's not attractive." He turned and left the room.

A part of her wanted to follow, to yell at him, to make him feel the entirety of her frustration and disbelief and anger, but she felt so wrung out and empty. She sat on the bottom step of the stairs and stared into the distance until she regained the strength to walk up to her bedroom.

Chapter Fifteen

Troy was hesitant to walk through the door of his own bedroom, and it was utterly ridiculous that he felt that way.

He shouldn't be nervous. They hadn't exactly fought, after all. Yes, Adele had been angry at him—and at the world and at the natural order of things, but mostly at him—but they hadn't fought in the traditional sense of the word. Mostly because he hadn't responded. But it was semantics.

At last he decided to knock on the door. There was no answer.

"Della … it's me. Can I come in? I just want to talk a bit."

Still only silence greeted him.

"Della, I love you so much." He paused. "I don't think you can even comprehend how much you mean to me. Every day, I thank God I have you. Please, don't let this come between us. Come on. We'll get through this."

He thought he heard the bed squeak slightly.

"I … Della, I'm sorry. I was a bit angry earlier, and it was wrong of me. But I adore you. *J'taime, Madame* Kee, if you remember the French we've been going over." He smiled. He liked to think she was smiling a bit, too.

"And I think you ought to know—" His voice broke a bit, but he cleared his throat and soldiered on. "I think you ought to know that if you want to put the baby up for adoption, I'll do it."

He'd battled with it all day, but at last he'd come to the conclusion that ultimately her happiness meant more than his—and that, should the baby be given a proper family, it didn't particularly … well, it did matter, but at least he'd be able to find a proper family for it.

If he lost Adele over this, the baby wouldn't have a proper family, and he wouldn't have a wife.

He heard light footsteps cross the room, and she opened the door. "Come in. It's your room, too." She left him standing in the doorway and paced back to the bed. "It's not … well, I've been thinking. It's not your fault, Troy. I've always known it wasn't, but I got so mad, and I wasn't even sure why."

His heart lightened. Perhaps that was even an understatement; he felt like a huge chain had suddenly been tossed aside, and he was able to breathe freely again. "It's all right. I understand. You were just … frustrated."

"Yes, well." Adele sighed and ran a hand over face. "I don't … I don't want to make you give up the baby. I know you want it."

"I want you more." Yet it would be such a blessing, such a beautiful blessing to have this baby.

If only Adele would let him, he'd be the best father in the world—and the best husband, too.

"Yes, but I think … I think both of us ought to try to make the other happy. And I know this would make you happy." Adele twisted her hands together. "Perhaps we can try. See how it goes."

Troy nodded. "That sounds nice to me. Let's see how it goes." *You're going to break my heart if you change your mind about the baby, though, Adele, so walk carefully.* Yet he couldn't say that to her. He loved her. He wanted her to be happy—even if it meant tearing his own dreams to shreds and dancing over the torn pieces.

"I'm going to love the baby very much," he admitted softly, crossing the room and wrapping his arms around her. "I do already. But I'll also always love you."

"I know."

She didn't say, "I'll always love you, too," and for the first time, it bit at the back of his mind even as he held her.

He shouldn't mind. It shouldn't matter. Yet it did. It mattered that she should be able to look him in the eye and tell him she loved him.

He didn't believe in fanciful things, that romance was the only thing that mattered or that one's emotions should control what one did. He thought love was more of an action.

Yet Adele wasn't so good at performing that action. And the more he thought about it, the more he wondered if her inability to say the words more than every so often—and usually when things were light and not stressful—had something to do with that.

He was the one who bent and bent until he was sure he'd break, lose his morals and his thoughts and opinions to be with her. He wouldn't do that. There was a limit. There was, moreover, a God.

And he'd firmly believed ever since he'd found out she wasn't a Christian that he could convert her—but what if he spent the rest of his life married to a woman who couldn't understand his ideals, his morals, his thoughts, the very center of his soul?

What if he raised children who were forever torn between one parent and the other? What if the little baby Adele carried now couldn't decide between his or her father's faith and mother's lack of religion? What if she chose to give up completely and become atheist or convert to some obscure eastern religion or something?

Anything could happen.

He sat on the edge of the bed and let Adele hold on to him. She didn't cry, but she was trembling. Scared. Scared because to Adele, having a baby was more frightening than facing down a man with a gun or spiders or any of the other things that most women trembled at.

Why, just by chance, couldn't the woman he loved be the kind who cried with joy when she found out she was pregnant? That was what his mother had reportedly done on each instance of finding out she was expecting—wept, because she'd been too happy, too excited.

Adele wasn't that kind of woman, though. She was the kind of woman who sat stiffly in his arms yet didn't want him to leave because she was frightened of being a mother. Of having his baby.

Because she didn't want to start a family with him.

Perhaps there was something about him that made her feel that he was unworthy to be a father? No. No, that couldn't be. She loved him. Of course she loved him. It was just because she was Adele, and Adele didn't want a baby.

And that was all right. He could adjust to that. To the fact that, assuming she adjusted to motherhood at all, this would be their only child.

Adele looked up at him. "Troy?"

"What, Della?"

"I know you don't understand at all, but I believe you're trying to understand. And I believe you love me even though I've said things that to you must be hateful. And I appreciate that. I love that you are a kind, caring, loyal man in spite of it all. In spite of the fact that I just don't … don't see things the way you do in many ways, and I know I've … disappointed you. With my attitude about this, I mean."

"Della, no, I just—"

"Shush. It's all right." She kissed his cheek and smiled. "You're my good angel. I don't need my good angel to apologize for being good."

Chapter Sixteen

Christmas 1931
French Riviera

Why was it that something that brought so much joy could be so exhausting? Christmas was all very well and good, but there were times when Adele wished she could curl up in a ball and sleep for a week. Or go to her bedroom and cry. Either way.

"Doing all right?" Troy took a seat next to her on the sofa and slid his arm around her shoulders. "You look droopy."

Adele leaned her head against her husband's shoulder. "I want to go to sleep," she whispered.

"Then do! Take a nap. We don't mind." He gestured to the small group of people scattered about the living room. "Honestly, do you think any of them are going to begrudge you some rest on Christmas Eve?"

"I don't want to be the Scrooge of the family." She glanced at her watch. "We're going to eat in half an hour."

"We'll postpone." He kissed her cheek. "Don't worry. You're not a Scrooge; you're a mother."

You're a mother. The words echoed tauntingly off the insides of Adele's mind, driving her wild, but she forced herself to smile in spite of it all. Millie, Lola, and Dave all expected Adele to be ecstatic over the coming child. Well, at least Lola and Dave did; Millie probably knew, or suspected, her true feelings.

Lola, on the other hand, was joyful over the prospect of being an aunt—and Dave seemed enthusiastic about unclehood, too. Adele had worried that Lola wouldn't be pleased, given that her sister-in-law actually wanted a baby and here Adele was having one when she didn't.

That was part of the reason why she felt it best to make believe she wanted to have Troy's child. She didn't want to make Lola hate her entirely; it was best to stay on good terms.

"So?" Troy nudged her. "Going to nap?"

Adele nuzzled his neck. "I think so. Just for a bit. Wake me in half an hour, though; I'm serious about dinner. I don't want you to starve."

Troy stood and helped her to her feet. "What a sweetheart you've become! Mother instinct, I must assume?"

Adele rolled her eyes. "I don't think you have to have a lot of mother instinct to not want someone to die slowly and horrifically." She turned and left the room.

It was odd; she'd felt as if she were falling asleep on the sofa, but now she couldn't sleep in her own bed. She tossed and turned a bit, then ended up giving up and simply laid there staring at the ceiling.

The baby was an undeniable fact now. She was starting to show, so much so that even a loose sweater did a poor job hiding it, and the little thing moved about inside her, too. She wasn't sure if that was disconcerting or not. Troy thought it was exciting.

Troy thought everything about the baby was exciting.

Millie was the same way. She'd come last week, deciding the opportunity to spend the holidays in France was not to be missed, and had spent the whole time rattling on about baby names, what color eyes it would have, whether it'd be a boy or a girl, and what color they should paint the nursery. Adele hadn't thought about any of those things, and she answered as vaguely as she could.

Eventually Millie had grown very quiet and then changed the subject. Which was why Adele was sure she knew—or at least partially knew.

Her mother didn't know. That much she was sure of. Adele had fooled her mother, who had only arrived yesterday, by being exceedingly loving with Troy, forcing herself to bring up the baby on occasion, and showing her mother where the nursery would be built on this spring after things dried out a bit.

Mother had actually been rather excited. She hadn't directly spoken to Adele about it, but she wasn't trying to hide her pride in the idea of being a grandmother. She'd even spoken with Troy on the subject several times in the last twenty-four hours—which, of course, Troy had reported back to Adele.

It was so odd that cold and calculated Mother

should be so excited about her coming grandchild, but Adele supposed that every woman had their weakness. Mother's must be children. Or, at least, children that weren't Adele. Adele's was flowers. It was a much less expensive and time-consuming weakness.

Flowers were simple. They got watered every once in a while, they got put in the sunshine, one dug around their roots on occasion. But never had she changed a flower's nappy or got up at 2 AM with it.

Flowers never rebelled against one. Flowers never thought one was an old woman who didn't understand them. Flowers didn't go away. Even when they died, one just grew more. Flowers couldn't yell or cry or hate.

Flowers weren't capable of feeling pain. Flowers weren't likely to be hurt by one's actions. Flowers wouldn't be friends—but neither would they be enemies.

Flowers were a lot less of a commitment than babies.

Adele wiped at her suddenly damp face with the back of her hand. What was wrong with her? Crying over flowers. How silly. She had more important things to think about than whether or not a flower was going to hurt her.

"Della?" Troy peeked his head in. "You said to wake you in half an hour, and I know you meant it."

Adele sat up and turned to face him.

He stared at her for a moment before speaking. "Della, have you been crying?"

"Oh! Well, you know I get emotional."

"Yes, but what were you emotional about?" He crossed the room and took a seat on the edge of the bed. "Are you sure you're okay?"

"Of course, of course!" She smiled. "Don't you worry. Baby and I are doing fine."

"How can you know that? I really think we ought to schedule another doctor appointment. What if something's wrong? What if Baby isn't doing well or you aren't doing well? Also, I wonder if you can find out—"

"Troy, no matter how many times you ask, I can assure you that no doctor is going to be able to tell if it's a boy or a girl short of cutting me open and taking a peek. Also, I will not be going to back-to-back doctor appointments. I'm reasonably sure this is a natural thing which I shall survive. And I feel fine." Better than she had for the first couple months, at least. Those had been miserable.

"Yes, well." Troy sighed. "I just want to make sure you're as safe as I can make you. Sometimes you can't tell with these things. Maybe Baby's not doing well. I mean, you're not showing a lot. Maybe Baby's supposed to be growing a bit faster—" He cocked his head to the side. "Or slower. Honestly, I don't know, but a doctor sure would. So—"

"Troy. No. No doctors for another month or so." She reached up and pulled his head down for a kiss. "You'll see. It'll all come out right in the end. And you'll have a beautiful little son or daughter."

Beautiful. Our child will be beautiful ... and loved. I—we—can do this. We can be parents. We can raise a child.

She took a deep breath and swung her legs over the edge of the bed. "Now for dinner, darling. I'm sure the rest want to eat, too—goodness knows I do."

~

Adele loved the homey atmosphere of the house that Christmas morning. Everyone was getting along well—even the Coles and Mother, something that surprised her. She'd thought her mother hated all strangers.

Perhaps she was only making an exception for the in-laws, though Adele wasn't sure why. Everyone seemed to be making an extra effort to be pleasant, and of course Troy was good with everyone, Millie was accustomed to Mother, and Adele didn't mind any of them—except perhaps her mother.

Even her mother wasn't such a trial this Christmas, though. It was like she'd been sanded down and smoothed out into a much gentler version of herself. Still stiff, still endlessly proper and moralistic, but not so harsh and abrasive.

She even offered Adele a somewhat awkward hug. Adele pulled back as soon as she feasibly could without it seeming odd to Lola and Dave, but it didn't change that Mother had willingly touched her daughter in an affectionate manner for the first time in she didn't know how long. Ages, it seemed.

It was like she was trying to redeem herself. Well, she wouldn't succeed. All Mother had said and done had made her irredeemable to Adele, and she would never, never forgive her. Not for a hundred hugs and a thousand pleasant days.

Still, it was nice having a family. Nice being able to count on some people for safety, security, that sense of oneness and unity. Nice that she was bringing a child into a place where it'd be loved, even if it was a wild, undependable world.

Chapter Seventeen

December 31st, 1931

"It seems like just a little bit ago I was curled up with Millie in our apartment sipping tea, munching on crackers and cheese, and waiting for midnight," Adele commented dreamily. She leaned her head against Troy's shoulder as they sat on the sofa alone for the evening since Harrington had already toddled off to bed. "I can't believe a year has gone by. Now I'm married with a baby coming in June."

"This is a surprise for me, too." Troy kissed her forehead. "I'm so excited to begin this new chapter with you."

A new chapter. That was what it was, she supposed. A new chapter of her life as *Madame* Kee, a wife and mother, a housekeeper and homemaker. She wasn't sure if she wanted more from her life or was simply growing restless under the weight of the commitments this kind of thing would force her to keep until the end of eternity, but whatever the reason, it chafed.

“So, have we thought about names? I know Millie was bothering you about it.” Up until the moment she’d left, Millie had been asking baby questions, though slightly subdued due to Adele’s disinterest. Adele had carelessly confided that to Troy, who was now making naming their child pre-birth his number one priority.

“Oh, Troy, let’s leave that.”

“No, really. What do you think? Come on. I know someone as opinionated as you must have an idea.” He playfully kissed her neck.

Adele laughed. “I have an idea for one name, I suppose. I’d … I’d like to call our son Kenneth Judah. I don’t care if it’s a girl too much—I hope it’ll be a boy, honestly. Little girls are so difficult. I ought to know; I was one.”

Troy smiled. “Actually, I rather like little girls. I’ll welcome one … but a son would be glorious, too. Honestly, any child with you would be glorious. But don’t think I’ve a thing against a bouncing baby girl.”

“I know you haven’t. But I do.” Girls were trouble, plain and simple, and so much more complicated than the male half of the race. Men she could deal with, but she wasn’t so good with women. It would be better for it to be a son. And that way Troy would have an easier time fathering him. No matter what the conceited man thought, it must be easier for a man to parent another little man than a little woman.

“All right, then. A boy it is.” He kissed her neck again—she’d been turning her head away so he couldn’t touch her mouth for several months now, and it had gotten to be a habit of his—then cocked his head. “And where will we be having this strapping son of mine?”

“A hospital, of course.” Even traditional Troy wouldn’t expect her to have her baby at home like an animal.

“Yes, but where? There’s the hospital in the town, but would you rather us stay in Paris? Or London? Or —?”

“The hospital in town will do, I think. It seems quite modern.” Actually, she’d stopped by a few weeks ago to have a chat with the nurse. She wanted to make sure they were forward-thinking and wouldn’t object to the use of anesthesia. She’d been told childbirth hurt—most women said a lot, even if they were trying to be brave about it—and she wasn’t about to feel it if it could be prevented.

“All right, then. So that’s settled.” He wrapped an arm about her and glanced down. “So you’re content? You’ll have the baby and bring it home to this house? And you’ll be fine with the nursery I’m building on? And you can keep the baby in our room for a few months?”

“Yes, yes, yes, and yes again.” Adele smiled. “Don’t worry. We’ll do fine. I’m sure the nursery will turn out well, and I’ve read that a baby ought to be with its mother at first.” She planned on using formula—again, she wasn’t an animal, but rather a woman, and she considered breastfeeding rather barbaric—but at least she wanted to hear it cry so she could get a bottle. Or Troy could. Either way.

“But what if we have a girl?” Troy asked after a long comfortable silence. “Shouldn’t we think of a girl name, too?”

Adele shook her head. "We'll cross that bridge if we come to it. Don't worry. We don't have to be quite that prepared." She kissed his cheek.

He was content, pressed a kiss to her forehead and tucked her into his side. As always, his hand wandered on down to rest on the baby bump. Adele even let it remain for a moment before brushing it away.

Troy was terrible about asking if she was comfortable with him randomly putting his hands on her body. It was like the baby had diserrected all barriers in that area. It wasn't to be borne, even from Troy.

~

Why didn't she want him to touch her?

Troy didn't understand it. Ever since she'd become pregnant, Adele had been remarkably hands-off. And yes, he understood it to a certain extent, as far as not risking hurting the baby or some such, but kissing should be all right—and so should hugging and snuggling and all those sorts of caresses.

He supposed she was punishing him for some crime he hadn't committed—at least, he hadn't committed it by himself—but it was still hard on him. Especially since he loved her more than anything—especially since it wasn't as easy for him to shake off loyalty as it apparently was for her.

He'd been living in a fantasy dreamland for the last six months or so, ignoring responsibilities, dropping the vineyard, focusing on her. Letting their financial situation go to ruins.

He was going to have to work double time to catch up and have the nursery ready for Baby, but he knew it'd be worth it. If he could get through this rough patch, they'd be almost home free.

Almost. Times were tough and getting tougher. Tourism was stalling, which meant less restaurants were buying wine. However, he'd just have to widen his horizons a bit—find new buyers if he had to.

After all, he was a family man. And family men took care of their own. He'd make a way to support his wife and child if it was the last thing he did.

Even, he thought guiltily, if it meant he wouldn't be at home so often when his pregnant wife needed him most. And probably after the baby came, for a year or two, he'd still be scrambling. But it would be worth it. Even Adele must see that. Or at least he'd convince her somehow.

But he'd talk to her about it later. Right now she'd fallen asleep cradled against his shoulder. He lay there staring into the darkness and holding her well into 1932.

Chapter Eighteen

June 1932

June was too hot a month to be having a baby in. There was no denying it, and Adele did not appreciate Troy's comment that July or August would have been even hotter.

Besides, it was unseasonably warm that particular June—or perhaps she just wasn't used to the Riviera. Whatever the reason, Adele was utterly miserable, and she wanted this whole ordeal to be over.

It had been going on too long already. Honestly, couldn't the length of pregnancy be shorter? A few months would surely be sufficient; the baby just had to learn to grow a bit faster.

What did Troy mind if she was melting away in the cramped little house on the vineyard? He'd been on business trips through half of the pregnancy, it seemed, and was always working when he was home.

It just wasn't fair. He didn't care about her anymore. He was too busy for her. And here she was, about to have his baby.

At least he was here now. She glanced across the room from her current bed, the sofa in the living room. He'd thought to bring her lemonade and prop her feet up before he went back to his ceaseless accounting.

She sucked in a quick breath and half-pushed herself up. Across the room, Troy glanced at his watch.

"Twenty minutes." He was more thinking aloud than anything since Adele was resolute that she didn't want to discuss the time between contractions. It made her nervous. "Is it worse as far as pain?"

"It's more uncomfortable. And surprising. Rather more like a cramp than anything, though. A bit sharp."

"Hmm." Troy set his papers aside and shuffled across the room to the bookshelf where he'd stored a variety of books on midwifery which he'd been obtaining over the past months. Adele hadn't touched them, but Troy had pored over the textbooks in every spare second he had, usually when Adele was trying to sleep and having the light on was most inconvenient.

"I think that's normal," Troy said after scanning through several chapters.

"Well, I could've told you that."

"Don't tell me you've developed some motherly instinct." He winked at her.

"I'm not sure if that's it. I—" She paused and grasped the back of the sofa as another pain gripped her. Let her breath out as steadily as she could. Troy was at her side.

"It was worse that time, wasn't it? Should we get you to the hospital?" Troy gripped her hand and looked worriedly into her eyes.

"No … no." She sighed and rubbed her belly. "It's all right. That was closer, wasn't it?"

She wasn't sure if she was more excited it was over or terribly, terribly afraid. It was going to get a lot worse before it got even a little better—and even better was relative. Better meant a baby she was responsible for. Better meant she had to be a responsible, sane adult.

Better meant that she was going to be a mother.

Troy forgot about his accounting after that. He remained kneeling on the sofa next to her except for brief interludes when he returned to his midwifery books or paced to the telephone only for Adele to call him back, to tell him not to bother the nurse again until things started getting more intense.

The afternoon wore on. A slight breeze blew up from the sea through the open window and brushed over Adele's face. It was a kind of relief, a small one, and she offered Troy a smile.

"So when did she say we ought to go in?" she asked. She needed to get Troy's mind off her pains, or he'd probably explode.

"Ten minutes, I think—or was it five?" He half-rose.

"No, don't call her. What … what do your books … say?" She struggled through the sentence, bending her head forward and panting softly.

"Della?" His hand gripped hers. "Is it bad?"

"Yes," she gasped out. "Oh. What was that?"

"About twelve minutes. Do you think that's close enough? Should I drive you down?"

"Call the nurse … and ask. Tell her … tell her it's hard to bear. I … I rather want to make sure I'm under anesthesia for the worst." She huffed out a breath. "Why is it so slow? I thought it'd be over in a trice, and here we are waiting hours with no progress …"

Troy squeezed her hand. "I'll ring her up and ask if it's normal. Call me back if you have another contraction, all right? We need to keep track of things."

Adele didn't want to keep track of things. She just wanted to have the baby and be done with it. Just wanted to stop this terrible dread and fear and excitement and frustration. Just wanted the pains to end now before they became as bad as most women said they were. Already she felt weak from them; what must it be like if this were the easy part?

They left for the hospital half an hour later.

~

Slowly the buzzing in her head lightened and allowed her to return to consciousness.

Adele blinked and half-propped herself on her elbows before remembering where she was—in the hospital, in a glaringly white room. She dropped back on the somewhat flat pillow.

"*Madame* Kee?" A starch-pressed nurse entered the room, clipboard in hand. She rattled off a string of French words.

Adele raised her eyebrows. "What?"

"Ah! I'd forgotten. I said, are you well?"

"I … I'm not sure." Adele pressed a hand to her forehead. "My head is buzzing."

"*Naturellement*." The nurse crossed the room, eyes on her clipboard. "It will pass soon. How else do you feel?"

"I don't know." She supposed the ether would ease after a bit, but for now, she didn't feel all too well. Her head felt full, and when she moved it, nausea took over.

"Also *naturellement*." The nurse was smiling. "You'll be good in no time. In fact, I can probably bring your *bébé* to you."

Oh, right. There was a baby now. Adele shook her head. "I'd … I'd rather not see it, actually. I just … I need a bit more time." She rested her head against the pillow and closed her eyes.

A bit more time to process her mess of a life. A bit more time to decide how she felt about things. A bit more time to cope with the endless pretending she must carry on in the coming years and decades if she was going to pull off "devoted wife and mother." A bit more time for her head to stop buzzing.

"Ah." The French nurse cocked her head but didn't say a word. "Well, this will *te remonter le moral*. Cheer you up, I mean. *Monsieur* Kee is waiting to see you, *Madame*. I told him myself he could come home and sleep, that you wouldn't be up until this morning, but '*Non*,' he says. 'You never know with these things. I'll stay here.' *Un homme fidèle, Madame. Très chanceux*. You, I mean."

Adele didn't understand much of that, but she got the idea. "Yes … yes, I know. But why don't you try telling him to go home again? Tell him I said to. Insist."

The nurse cocked her head. "Why would you want to send him away? *Il vous aime*. Why wouldn't you want to see a man who … I don't know how to express it." She pursed her lips. "I just know you don't send it home."

Adele didn't respond. The nurse sighed and walked out of the room.

A kind of self-hatred began boiling in her chest. Why couldn't she be loving to Troy? Why couldn't she want him? Yet she just didn't feel like listening to his joy and sweet words and gentleness.

He would be kind and lovely and understanding … and she couldn't stand it. A few of the words of the nurse were easily translated, even by her—'A faithful man who loves you.' Indeed, Troy was that.

But he was also the man who held her to tradition and now the baby. The man who stood to take any chance of happiness from her.

It wasn't fair, really. She hadn't known all this would happen when she married him. She hadn't known she'd end up lying flat on her back in a hospital bed feeling like her body had fallen apart.

What had happened to the slim, happy, fun woman of a year ago? Less than a year, even. She was gone—but Adele wanted to be that girl again. Wanted to dance all night and have the freedom to flirt with any man she wanted to and drink as much as she wanted.

Now she was fat and ugly and aching all over.

It just wasn't fair.

A tear trickled down her cheek as she considered a life that felt wasted. She couldn't believe it—twenty-three and already a mother, already tied to one man for life, already settled.

It was inhumane. Old-fashioned.

Nauseating.

Yet she must. She couldn't hurt Troy; she just couldn't. Not after he'd been so good to her. Not after this was her dream romance.

She'd just have to try again; she'd just have to capture the feelings she'd experienced before. Somehow. Perhaps they weren't gone for good.

~

Troy crossed the room in two great strides and knelt beside the hospital bed, stretching his arms around her.

"*Ma belle mariée, ma belle* Della," he whispered into her hair. "Have you seen her? Have you held her? They won't let me yet."

"I haven't."

"Really? How awful! They should let a mother see her own child. Now, what did I tell you about hospitals? But it's all right; I'll make them bring her in. I've seen her through the window. She's beautiful, *ma belle*.

"Oh, and Della, she's going to have red hair, I think! Oh, Della, imagine! I wouldn't have thought it in a million years. She's so precious. Has all her fingers and toes and ears and a little nose … I can't believe she's ours!"

He was aware he was babbling but didn't care. He

needed to communicate this joy to someone, and no one else was willing to listen. Hospital staff were unsympathetic, and Harrington, who had stopped by late last night to check in on them, had simply rolled his eyes.

But Adele must understand. She was the mother, after all. She must love the baby as much as he did—which, he thought, was a brilliant design of God's, to make two people who loved one person so much.

It would be a tough kind of love to experience without someone to talk to about; he knew that from experience. Of course, it would be better once he had a little baby to hold and snuggle and take care of, but it was going to be even better with Adele.

"I don't see why you haven't thrown a fit," Troy said. He about had, but it hadn't done a bit of good—still, a mother should be given priority. "I know you've only been awake for a bit, but it'll be good for you to hold her. You seem to be a bit under the weather, but I know holding the baby will perk you right up. Oh, Della, I can't wait until you see her! She's so beautiful."

"It's a baby girl?" Adele said.

Troy blinked. "They didn't even tell you that? Why, they told me first thing."

"I … I was under the ether, and then when I woke up I … I didn't think to ask."

Troy stared at her for a moment then chuckled. "Della, you're such a silly goose sometimes." He squeezed her arm. "That's the first thing you want to find out! Yes, it's a glorious baby girl, and I can see bits of you in her, I think, but it'll be good to get a closer peek. Like I said, her hair is light, and I think it'll be red, and I just …" He stopped for a moment and grinned. "Well, I can't explain it. Let me bring her in, dearest. I'll talk them into it." He half-rose.

"No."

Troy paused. Her voice sounded like glass crashing to the floor, and he had no idea why. "What do you mean?"

"No, I don't want to see her. Of course I don't. She's turned me into an ugly pig, after all, hasn't she? Why would I want to see the little beast? Besides, I wanted a boy, not a girl."

An empty place swelled in his chest then was quickly filled by a rush of anger. He turned away from her, walked to the window, and stood there. His chest rose and fell quickly, but he kept his face as clear as he could. She couldn't know. He'd restrain himself, and somehow … somehow they'd get through this together.

"You're not an ugly pig, Della," he said without turning to face her. "You're a lovely woman, face and form. There's not a thing about the baby which has changed that. You're … to me, Della, you look more beautiful every day, and when I walked into this room this morning, I thought, 'doesn't she look like an angel?' And I meant it. I always mean it."

He turned to her, but she wasn't looking at him. She was staring at the wall, hands twisted in her lap, eyes distant.

"Della?" He sat on the edge of the bed. "Della, look at me."

"I don't want to. I don't want to … I don't want to do this. Troy, I don't want the baby. Look. There's … there's an orphanage here in town, isn't there?"

It was impossible to keep the fury in check this time. "Don't you dare, Della! Don't you dare." He grabbed her shoulder and yanked her to face him. "If you think you're going to let me fall in love with my daughter and then whisk her away, you're wrong. I'd do anything for you except that."

"Of course! Because when it comes to this baby, you can guarantee that whatever is best for it will come before what's best for me!" Adele pushed hard against him then moaned and dropped her head back.

"Della! What?"

"Oh, shut up, Troy. You don't care!"

"Of course I care, darling." He was mad, but he wasn't an insensitive idiot. If she was hurting, that came first and the fight second. In fact, why were they even starting to fight? They wouldn't, they couldn't.

"So what is it? Did they have to operate or …?" He really wished he knew more about childbirth, but he'd have to hope that Adele had a better grasp on the subject—it was happening to her, after all.

"No. I'm just sore, and my head is throbbing. I feel sick."

"It's probably the anesthesia."

"Oh, let's not start that again!"

Troy sighed. "All right, I won't. But Della—"

"Let's not talk if we're going to fight."

"I'm not going to fight! If you can keep yourself from that, we'll get through this without a cross word, I promise. Let's just work on this together a little, Della—let's promise each other we will fight through it."

Adele didn't respond. She just stared ahead of her with blank eyes and let him stand there with his eyes half-closed. What was happening? He couldn't believe this. Her coldness, her lack of concern over her own child, her unresponsiveness to his words … what had happened to his beautiful Della? His lovely Della, his sweet Della, *l'amour de sa vie*.

"Shall I leave you?"

A quick jerk of a nod.

"Very well, then." He turned toward the door then paused and glanced over his shoulder.

"Della, I love you very much. More than I ought to, I think. But I'm sorry—you can't push me any further. I must believe that someday you'll thank me for protecting our daughter, even from her mother's selfishness. I must believe that you're simply depressed, or it's the anesthesia, or … or something, something has caused my *belle* Della to act this way. So I will leave now, but I'm not giving up on us. I'll fight for us, and I hope that, in time, you'll be willing to fight, too."

She didn't so much as incline her head. Her face was stony and set, and he knew it was no use to speak further.

"I'll see you in a bit, *mon amour*," he said softly as he left the room.

Chapter Nineteen

Adele stared listlessly at the scenery as the shiny silver car rolled up the driveway between rows of grapes. Harrington had come down to drive them so Troy could hold his daughter on the way home.

Even now, her husband was sitting in the back seat making an utter fool of himself cooing over the ugly little thing.

Not that Adele had first-hand experience of the child's ugliness. So far, she'd managed to avoid no more than a quick glance on their way out of the hospital.

You're a coward, Adele. You know if you look you'll fall in love. You know you're afraid of your own heart betraying you.

Yet it would hurt so much when her daughter looked her in the eyes and told her she hated her. It would hurt so much when her daughter betrayed her, chased dreams Adele couldn't comprehend.

It would hurt so much when Adele wasn't enough for the baby. When the baby was hurting because of Adele.

And if she didn't love it, well, maybe she wouldn't hurt quite so bad. Maybe she'd be able to get through it without feeling like a piece of herself was ripped out and stamped upon.

"I think she smiled," Troy said.

"It's gas," said Harrington.

"Oh, stop being such a pessimist."

"Only when you stop being such an optimist." Harrington highlighted this with a determined punch to the gas pedal.

"Harrington!" Troy's voice was firm. "Slowly! Precious cargo—must I remind you again?"

Harrington just snorted. Adele couldn't help but smile a bit.

"I'm sure we'll all survive the last hundred yards, Troy," she said.

Troy mumbled under his breath then returned to getting to know his baby girl. Adele was almost jealous of his single-mindedness. He'd never been so in love with her; he'd never admired her the way he admired the baby.

It was like he didn't even remember she existed. And yes, she'd been difficult, and loving her would be the opposite of loving the baby at the moment—Troy would be crazy not to see that. Still, she pouted.

He'd made his choice. The baby was his choice, not Adele. She was secondary to the child now. Secondary to someone who had only been in the world a few days, whom he barely knew.

The car jerked to the stop with such suddenness that Adele could feel the gears moan in agony. She glanced at Harrington, and for the first time she saw him smile as Troy gave him a sound berating.

"And I can forgive you a lot of things, Harrington, but killing my daughter is not one of them," he ended with a huff as he stepped out of the car. "Redeem yourself and get Della's bag for me, please."

Harrington shrugged and grabbed the satchel which she'd been living out of since the child's arrival, and the two men went into the house. Adele stood there by the car for a moment, considering driving off a cliff and into the comfort of nothing.

But that was the coward's way out. She raised her chin and marched up the steps of the house. She wasn't beautiful any more, the body she prized distorted by a baby who was doing no one any good. Just taking Troy away from her.

This isn't what it's supposed to be like. He's supposed to side with me. Understand what a terrible strain this is on my nerves ... understand that I never wanted this.

Troy had already moved to the living room and was showing the infant around.

"And that's the view from the living room—and these are the curtains in the living room. Your mother picked them out, you know, just a few months ago. Take notice; this is your home."

Adele sighed. "She's too little to understand you, Troy."

"I know." Troy grinned. "But I can't help it. You know, Della, you can't understand until you hold her how much you'll love her. Trust me. You should give it a try."

Hadn't she just told herself why she mustn't love the baby?

"Judy is such a perfect little angel." Troy cuddled the bundle close and walked to sit down on the sofa. "My perfect girl."

After Adele had told him she wouldn't bother thinking about it, Troy had named their daughter Judith Ann Kee—Judith because it sounded rather like Judah and Ann because, as he said, "simplicity is always better."

Adele still wasn't used to hearing the baby referred to by her name. It made her so much more … real. Like an actual person instead of the creature she'd somehow managed to bring forth from her body despite her own reluctance.

"You act like the beast is the cleverest thing in the world when really she's just an ugly, filthy little baby —and unwanted at that! I wish I'd never had her—and I wish you'd let me give her to someone now. Someone who actually cares about her."

She didn't know what she was saying, really; only that she wanted to draw some sort of response from him, to shake that ever-present good-natured cheer. She saw the tendons in his neck tighten, but he closed his eyes, took a deep breath, then focused in on the baby once more.

This made her angry. He wasn't going to fight with her, was he? Well, she'd show him.

"Honestly, Troy, can't you grow up? What's wrong with you? Look at me. Don't be a coward."

"I'm not … not a coward."

"Then why won't you face your own wife when she's speaking to you?"

Troy raised his eyes to her face. "Because my own wife has become more hateful than I could have imagined. Because she's become cruel, unfeeling, and selfish, and because she's taken to attacking an innocent child—her own child—and I can't understand it. Maybe because I don't want to hurt you; maybe because I believe hurting a woman would be cowardly. But God knows if ever a woman deserved to be beaten, Della—"

Her stomach tightened. "Don't you threaten me."

"I'm not, Della. Not threatening—warning." Blue eyes turned steely gray. "There's only so far you can go. I'm patient; I'm forbearing, even, and I would never hurt you. That's not how I was raised. But if you're not going to at least pretend that you can be a decent human being, I will put you out of the baby's life."

She blinked. And let him have control? No. Never. He couldn't have control; she must be in charge. In charge of her life—and because he was so inexplicably tied to her, in charge of his. And now the baby. No, she mustn't lose control of the baby.

"You can't! I'm the mother, and you've no legal grounds. Do you want a divorce? Because you know they won't let you keep her. If you lose me, you lose the baby."

Troy went pale, and a muscle at the corner of his eye ticked. "Della, I never said I wanted a divorce. I never would say that! Why, you know—"

"I don't know anything anymore, Troy. I don't know who I am or who you are. You're threatening to beat me! I didn't even know you had a temper."

"I'm not going to beat you, Della! That's exactly why I'm not engaging; I'm not letting my temper get the worst of me. Look, I want to believe—I must believe—that we'll get past this—"

"You talk about moving past things that you refuse to face like a man!"

"I'm facing them the only way I know how to, Della—with sense and reasoning and maybe a bit of love."

"If you loved me, we wouldn't be keeping the baby."

Troy's jaw clenched. "You agreed—"

"I was foolish! I thought love meant more than this worry about the baby. But we don't love each other anymore, do we?"

She was desperate for an answer; desperate for him to do something that would assure her that she was in love with him, madly so—that of course it was still Troy, Troy whom she loved and treasured, and of course he loved her in return. That his love was still of the blind, puppy-dog variety, and hers still of a worshiped queen to her subject. That's what she wanted.

But that wasn't his response. Not devotion without knowledge or truth. Not even unending devotion.

"Of course I love you," he said. "I love you very much. But, Della, if you think love is all about giving in to you and you alone until you destroy us both, well—"

"Oh, shut up, Troy." She paced to the window and stared out. "I don't know what happened. I thought you actually cared about me, but really, you're just like any other man. You want to settle down and make me into a baby-producing machine, want me to pander to your every whim. You're selfish; you don't care about how I feel. You'll just leave when it gets hard. Just like every man, you're not devoted when devotion counts."

Was it ever real? Did I ever want this man? For in that moment, she hated him. Hated that he would force her to come out of her shell and be real; hated that he wanted her to offer more than a pat on the head and the privilege of serving her.

Hated that he was asking … asking for real love. Unselfish love. The kind of love she couldn't fathom. Why? Why must he? Didn't he know that she couldn't bear it?

He didn't know, and he didn't care. Selfish, selfish man. He must have it his way. Well, he wouldn't—couldn't.

Troy rose and left the room. Adele followed him.

"Where are you going?"

"Away from you," he said shortly. He walked into their room where the bassinet waited and carefully laid the baby in it. The tiny creature made some sort of fussing sound; Troy knelt and shushed her softly. At last, he rose and turned to Adele.

"I'm going for a walk. She should sleep; at least, I think so." He glanced worriedly into the lace-trimmed crib then back at her. "Try not to smother her while I'm gone. I can promise that I won't be able to rein in my temper if you hurt her in any way."

Adele's heart clenched. Did he really think she'd kill their child? Wanting to give it away was one thing; wanting to kill it quite another. She shook her head. "I'll leave her be."

"Good." He brushed past her and down the stairs.

Adele went to sit on the edge of the bed and stare

moodily at the bassinet. Not long after Troy left, a rasp of a cry came from within, followed by some more hearty screams that indicated that help was wanted if not needed. Adele glanced around, hesitated, then stood and walked over.

There a child lay surrounded by a wealth of white. Her puckered and scrunched up face turned red and angry. No tears, just the needy cry that touched a place in Adele's heart that she hadn't known was there.

She blinked, took a step back, then one forward.

Now, what did the little thing want? Surely it wasn't hungry. The thing had just eaten at the hospital, and she'd thought the next bottle was at three; it was only two now.

Did it need its nappy changed? She'd heard that babies mostly cried for that or if they were tired. Troy had tried to talk to her about it, but she hadn't listened. She wished she had now.

Well, changing the baby might be a bit beyond her, but she could at least check to see if it was needed.

Somewhat awkwardly, she slid her hand behind the baby's head and back and lifted her. It was a bit strange, but overall, it wasn't a bad experience. A bit of shifting, and she got the baby in what she considered to be a comfortable holding position. At least, it was rather nice. Homey, as little sense as that made.

And, strangely enough, the baby quieted down after a bit of rocking. Adele cocked her head.

"So was that crying a *faux pas* to get held?" she asked the baby. "Sounds like your father. I mean, he never cries, but in the middle of summer on the Riviera, you're not cold; you're just a man."

The baby made no response save a bit of a sigh. Her eyes were closed now, and her head kept pressing against Adele's chest in a sleepy, trusting sort of way.

"But you're not supposed to trust me," she whispered. "I'm not trustworthy. I'll hurt you. Don't you know that?"

Small fingers found the fabric of Adele's blouse and tried to make a fist then clumsily failed. Adele moved her arm up to touch the perfect little digits.

"I suppose you don't know much of anything." She backed up to sit on the edge of the bed. "You're a bit new." Adele smoothed her fingertips over the baby's cheek. "That's all right. You're a bit new to being a baby, and I'm a bit new to holding one. But I think, given the practice we've had at our individual roles, we're doing quite well."

The baby stirred and yawned.

"Judy," Adele whispered. "It's all right, Judy. I've got you. It's Mother; you know you're safe with me, don't you?"

There was no response from her daughter, but Adele took her silence as confirmation. If the baby didn't feel safe, she'd make a noise again, or at least Adele thought so.

"Judy? What if … what if I was special to you? And what if I could take you away somewhere, and you … *you* could just love *me*?" Adele cocked her head. "If … if I were all you had, then you'd have to … have to stay, wouldn't you? If you were small and helpless, and I was your … your mother?"

No response from the baby.

"Judy, I think I'd like to maybe … I don't know. I want to go back to my own life. But that would mean leaving you. And I don't know about that anymore. I thought I did, I thought it would be easy, but now I feel as if …" Her voice trailed off as a sort of determination entered her heart. "Judy, I can't stay here anymore. I'm too hurt. I'm too … too tortured by your father. He's threatened me, he prioritizes you over me, and it seems like … well, he'll leave. Men always leave, baby. Don't you doubt it for a moment.

"But what if he didn't get a chance to leave? What if we didn't give him that satisfaction? What if, instead of him taking everything from us, we took everything from him?"

She liked that idea. She liked the idea that a man in her life wouldn't wreck it. She liked the idea that she would have control most of all. That she would hurt Troy, destroy his world, and still have control over the baby, over herself, and, because of those two controls, over her husband, too.

"Of course, I don't know that I want him to be my husband … but with you, well, he's still mine in a way."

It felt sick even as she told the baby it, and she was ashamed.

"I know you must not understand why I'd want it," she said guiltily. "It's just … well, it's so hard being a woman in this world, Judy. So very hard. And … I didn't think I'd involve other people in my life, especially men or my mother, but then I kept involving men, and I kept falling for them … and I thought Troy was a safe bet, but he didn't end up being. Nothing has gone as I wanted it to go. It hasn't made me happy to be with him.

"Being happy is important, baby. There's not much else in this world. Everything is able to be blown away in a moment, so the best you can do is try not to spend your life miserable. Try to spend it devoted to your own … your own pleasure."

Sick, said her conscience. *Sick, sick, sick.* But she pushed it down, pushed it back into the furthest parts of her soul.

"A baby is a world of possibilities. I couldn't control Troy; I couldn't make him into what I wanted him to be. But that's because he was already grown. Maybe you can grow up to be someone I can stand being around with a bit of effort."

At last, the baby opened her eyes, and Adele was sucked into an ocean of blue. Her heart stopped a moment as she looked into a reflection of her husband's face, and then the impression was gone, though the ghost remained behind.

She swallowed. "Pretty eyes you've got there," she said. "I did always like his eyes. How they sparkled and danced. How they made me want to smile when they were laughing."

The blue eyes blinked up at her, taking in the unfamiliar face. The little nose crinkled. She seemed to accept the woman above her and settled back in.

"I think you like me, too," Adele said firmly. "I think I'm going to like you an awful lot. Especially if you keep being such a good baby. Why, you're not particularly smelly, either, though I bet that'll change with the first soiled nappy. Still, nappies can be cleaned, and so can babies, and perhaps you'll always smell like newness and baby powder. I like that smell."

She also liked the little swish of red hair, the chubby pink cheeks, the tiny fingers which were individually perfect right down to miniscule fingernails, and the overall weight and shape of her.

"You're a good shape, I think. It's a good shape for someone to hold in their arms—meaning me, of course. Funny—just days ago you were inside me. What a funny thought! I suppose you fit in there, too. It was awkward, sometimes, and hateful, but it wasn't exactly a bad fit. I don't think."

Adele laid back against the pillow with Judy on her chest. She realized how sleepy and hungry she was, but she ignored that. She couldn't eat until she got her figure back, or at least not much. It made her weak and trembly, but it was worth it; some day she'd be Adele again, and men would look—but they couldn't *have*. No, she was done with men *having*, even if the only man she'd given herself to was Troy.

Poor Troy! How he'd want her … but he couldn't. Not again. No, and he couldn't have Judy, either. She was who he really wanted, but she wouldn't let him.

She laughed to herself as she drifted off with the baby close to her heart, where she belonged.

Oh, yes. Troy couldn't have the baby ...

Chapter Twenty

Three Weeks Later

Troy thought, or at least he hoped, that things were starting to look up between Adele and him. He'd taken a long walk that afternoon after bringing Judy home from the hospital, and when he'd come back, considerably cooled off, he'd found Adele sleeping on their bed with Judy cuddled close.

His heart had melted; he'd crossed the room, gathering them both into his arms, and covered both of his favorite girls in kisses.

Adele had pushed him away and told him to sleep in the nursery he'd constructed downstairs—but he'd felt hopeful. Even if she wasn't ready to reconcile with him, she was loving Judy, and that was enough.

Loving him must come as a matter of course, as they would love and work on raising Judy together. He'd be patient. He could love her like that.

Thank goodness whatever insanity had possessed her in the first days had passed!

He didn't want to push so much, so he waited for an invitation to return to his bedroom and only went in there to fetch clothes or Judy—the latter of which happened much more often. He never wanted to stop holding his baby girl.

Then he'd had to visit Paris to see that a shipment went off all right. He and Adele had gotten into a bit of a fight before he went; at least, she'd attacked him for always running off and leaving her alone with the baby.

He thought she might just be tired or something. That seemed the only reason for a woman to respond like that to a man's business trip where he would earn money for Judy's future—as well as their present.

But he'd regretted leaving angry, if only to catch his train, and he'd written her a note from Paris.

Dear Della,

I promised to write from Paris before our fight, so that's what I'm doing. I would call, but it's late, and the only times I have free are late at the moment.

So this is me telling you that I miss you so much that it hurts.

Is Judy all right? I miss her so much! Are her eyes darkening? I have mixed feelings about the color they take on. I want her to have my eyes, but I'd rather she had yours.

I know, I know. You've always said you wished you had blue eyes. They're a lot more romantic—blue skies and oceans and violets, et cetera.

But, you know, brown eyes have their advantages, too. For one thing, they're more sun-resistant. Also, chocolate. Besides, I think it's easier to fall into brown eyes. Such has been my experience.

Nonetheless, I may be able to love her if she resembles me. Or my sister. Lola called the other day and mentioned that she thought Judy is her mirror image from the photo we sent, which would please her immensely.

But I'm off-subject now. I've been thinking lately about our fight. Perhaps you're right. I have been spending a lot of time away from you recently.

But I thought you understood. You know how things are going to be. Children cost money. And not just food and clothing ... what about ponies and puppies and a trip to wherever she wants? And college? I want Judy to have all those things.

Besides, Della, even if you don't know it, times are hard. I'm having a difficult time keeping our heads above water. I wish you'd try to understand that.

I know you're used to getting what

you want when you want it, but that can't always happen. I wish I could make it happen—that's what I'm trying to do—but I can't. I'm not all-powerful.

So you've got to tell me how to make this right. I don't know how ... but I'm willing to try anything to restore your faith in me.

In closing, I can only say that I love you, and I'll crawl back on my knees if I have to. So forgive me, and when I get home, I'll stay, and if I have to leave again, I'll take you and Judy with me. We'll have a second honeymoon. It'll be fun.

With all the love in my heart,
Troy

He hoped that would pacify her. He wrote it sincerely. Really, it was hard to adore a woman who had stopped adoring him back, but he was going to stick to it and love her until she couldn't help but fall in love again.

Perhaps he was trying too hard to pretend things were normal and this was just a bit of a tiff. It was hard to tell. Yet he hoped they would ride it out. That it wasn't a huge issue. That it was only the upset with things changing so suddenly, with a baby causing them to rewrite their lives in major ways.

But it was a good kind of rewrite, and he knew the goodness would seep through the confusion and chaos brought on by Adele's refusal to try.

~

Harrington had gone to Angers to visit "an old friend"—Troy never inquired about Harrington's past, only accepted it—and Troy was rather looking forward to it just being Della, Judy, and him for a few days.

He should have known something was wrong when Holt came galavanting out to meet him. Holt was usually kept in the garage when Adele was home, so why would he be out now?

Troy jogged up the front steps and threw open the door.

"Della! Della, it's me. I'm home!"

Nothing answered him. He stood there for a second before realizing that the house was unnaturally still, save for Holt's thumping paws.

Where could she have gotten to that she didn't hear him? Or was she just pouting over his trip? If she'd gotten his letter, surely she'd listened to reason and was ready to make up.

Something odd filled his chest, a feeling he couldn't recognize. He cleared his throat as if that would banish the emotion and hastened his way up the stairs. He opened the door to the bedroom; no one there. Judy's bassinet was empty; the blankets had been stripped.

None of her possessions were lying around. Not even a loose sock. And Della was a big believer in leaving things as they laid, even if he did tend to trip over them, even if he hated clutter.

Was cleaning all her random things off the floor

and making everything so impeccably tidy her way of apologizing? He hoped so.

He turned from the room without giving it a second glance and went downstairs. All her possessions had similarly been removed from the living room; the kitchen was the same. Not even half a dozen fashion magazines. No teacups abandoned in the sink.

It was like she'd never been there.

Heart hammering, he called her name again. "Della? Della, I …" He couldn't explain it all in a shout. He went into the nursery, but things were untouched there. His clothing and other personal items still laid about as he'd left them. He backtracked quickly through the living room. He kept things impeccably neat, so he was immediately able to see the slip of paper lying on his desk.

It was folded in half with his name written in a messy cursive across the front. He picked it up and unfolded it.

> *Troy,*
> *I've decided to take Judy and go home to England …*

His vision went black, and he staggered back into his chair. What was this? This utter nonsense? Had he lost his mind?

He forced his eyes back to the paper.

> *It's not about you, so you needn't worry on that score. We just aren't compatible, and I don't think there's*

any use in fighting for something that was never there in the first place.

I didn't think a man like you would be equipped to care for a child, and honestly, I think the courts will side with me on this. You're welcome to fight it if you choose, but until then, I've decided that you can't see Judy.

His lips parted and a deep breath escaped him. *Can't see Judy.*

What did that mean? Of course he could see Judy. She was his baby girl … his sweet little angel, the only … the only creature he could love fully, and Adele couldn't, she wouldn't …

A low moan escaped his lips as he read on.

Please contact whomever handles your legal matters, and I will do the same.

I'm filing for divorce on grounds of neglect and threatened physical abuse—as well as the emotional impact said threats have had—and I don't really know what else.

I really do need to talk to a lawyer about this. I just know that I don't want to be involved with you any more.

Until then,
Adele Collier

It wasn't an angry letter. She hadn't given him

that satisfaction; the satisfaction of berating him and hurting him and making him feel like he could be defensive.

No, he couldn't be defensive to coldness and formality, to a woman who didn't care enough to show hatred. He could only sit there and take the blows, held down by invisible bullies as he took punch after punch to the gut.

Through the buzzing in his mind and the unbearable pain in his heart, two words escaped: *God, no. God, no.* More words came in time. *Please, no. Not my baby. Not my bride. Don't let them have left me. Please, God. I love them so. I need them so.*

Oh, God, I can bear anything else, but this will break me, and I can't ... I can't go on. No, God, please, God, not Della, not Judy, and not, not like this.

In a bit, he reasoned with it, he fought it. *I'll win her back. God, help me, help me win her back. Help me show her I love her, that we can fight for this, that it's worth fighting for. Help me, help me ...*

He dragged himself up and called her mother, looking for answers, but received no answer. He'd try again in the evening. Millie's apartment—no answer. She must be still at work. At last, weak and soulsick, he rang up his sister.

"Hello?"

At last, a familiar, beloved voice, someone who cared. "Lola. It's me."

"Troy?" Her voice was full of curiosity—but innocence. He could hang up now and spare her to pain.

"H-how are you, Lola?"

"I'm … I'm fine, Troy." Her voice was hesitant. "How about you?"

"I'm fine. I … I just got home from Paris."

"Oh?"

"Yes."

There was a moment of silence.

"Della's taken Judy and left me. She wants a divorce."

The silence stretched on even longer until Troy feared she'd fainted.

"Lola?"

"I'm still here." Her voice trembled. "Do you need me to come?"

"P-please."

"All right. I'll be there—probably not until late. I'm not sure Dave can follow tonight, but he'll try. Stay out of the liquor, all right?"

"Not sure I can."

"Sure you can. Just think about how mad I'll be if I get there and smell it on your breath. Where's Harrington?"

"Away."

"Angers?"

"Hmm."

"Troy, keep talking to me for a moment. What did she say?"

"Not much. A note. The house is impeccable. I wish … I wish the house weren't impeccable. When you get here, can you mess it up a bit?"

Somehow, she knew not to question it. "Sure, Troy. I can leave things everywhere; you know I'm best at it; better than she was, that selfish little—"

He knew what she wanted to call her, but he couldn't let her. Not within his hearing, at least. "Lola?"

"What?"

"I'm fighting the divorce, so she's still my wife."

A sigh. "All right, then, Troy. I'm hanging up now. Eat, please."

"Can't eat."

"Sure you can. Make yourself toast and eggs. I mean it."

"Can't, Lola. It'd make me sick."

"No, it won't." Her voice was stern. "Listen. I'm not letting you spiral. You wouldn't let me spiral. Troy? Listening?"

"Yes."

"I love you."

Yes. Yes, that was something he could hold on to."I … I love you, too."

"It's not your fault."

"How do you know?"

"Because I know you," she said softly. "It's going to work out. You'll see. God loves you, too, and this is all going to work out. I promise."

"I … I can't …"

"I know, Troy. It's okay to rebel a little, I think. Okay to ask why. Just know He understands better than anyone what it feels like to be spurned and hurt by those He loves most—because we spurn and hurt Him every day. But I know I shouldn't preach over the phone—I'm grabbing a few things first and calling Dave, and I'll be there. I promise. I'll see you."

"S-see you."

The receiver clinked, and Troy was desperately alone again.

Chapter Twenty-One

August 1932
London, England

There was nothing pleasant or welcoming about a courtroom, nor did Adele feel a sense of justice as she sat on the hard bench with Millie beside her.

Millie adjusted Judy on her lap and glanced at Adele. "When do things start?"

"Soon. Thanks for coming to mind the baby."

Millie smiled. "That's all right. I happen to love this little bundle of joy."

If there was one thing Adele knew for certain, it was that her best friend was absolutely baby-crazy. She loved cuddling, feeding, and even changing Judy. Adele thought she was a bit mad—but Millie didn't care.

Adele had gotten used to Judy, but that didn't mean that she wasn't frustrated with her on occasion. Especially when long, loud nights turned into fussy, fretful days.

So yes, having someone willing to do the heavy

lifting—not that Judy was heavy; just that taking care of her could get to be a bit of a burden—was a relief, especially when a much-needed nap came into play.

Judy fussed in Millie's arms. Adele reached for her purse, feeling like a mother more than ever as she withdrew a bottle and passed it to her friend.

It wasn't a big purse, but having a bottle in it was the first step. Having a ginormous bag hanging off her shoulder full of various odds and ends was the inevitable result.

"She probably wants to be fed," she mumbled.

Millie adjusted her hold on the baby. "Should I take her out?"

"Mm, I don't know." Adele shrugged. "Why don't you? She can fuss a bit afterwards, especially if she's sleepy."

Millie rose and skirted past Adele's knees before hurrying out of the small courtroom. It wasn't a big trial, but it would take some work to sway things in her favor. Even with the competent lawyer she'd hired.

For the first time, without Millie and Judy there to distract her, she allowed her eyes to stray across the room to a tall man sitting in a chair. He leaned so his back was to her as he spoke softly to a woman who looked very like him.

She wished he'd turn to her, if only for a moment. She needed to see his face—not because she cared, of course, but because she was curious to know how he was bearing up.

She knew she'd had nights when, as the early morning hours ticked away and Judy woke for no apparent reason, Adele had thought of him.

Wondered if this was the right choice. Wished he would come and beg her to take him back.

There had been nights when she imagined refusing him … and nights when she wanted to go to his arms and weep. When she would willingly bind herself to him again, when she would tell him to cancel the trial and take them home.

But it's not home, she told herself fiercely. *France is not home.* He *is not home.*

Yet on some nights he was, and then she was intensely homesick.

Adele had almost seen if she couldn't get a call across those nights, but the receiver had clinked back into its cradle before she'd even addressed the operator. She had to be strong through this. She'd gone too far to turn back now.

So yes, she ought to be glad that he didn't look at her. She probably couldn't have borne it. Couldn't have kept herself from going to his side and becoming too involved and raising his hopes—and, most of all, her own.

At last the trial began. Adele's lawyer was harsh, harsher than she'd felt he would be, spreading lies about Troy, about their marriage, about the conditions she'd lived in, about their life.

At times, she almost rose, almost called out, almost stopped him … but she couldn't. Not if she wanted this divorce.

Troy was going to fight it too hard for her to do anything but call him the worst sort of man, so she let her lawyer have at him.

And Troy didn't say a word.

Defeated. He looked defeated. His shoulders

slumped forward, his head bowed, hands clasped on the table in front of him. He took it all without a sound.

It took a lot of heart-hardening for her to stay away from him.

She did her best for him. Made it clear that he could come see Judy, that perhaps some sort of vacation schedule could be arranged as she got older. She offered summers and visitation, told him she'd make sure he could stay in contact. He showed no interest in it.

She'd broken him.

Adele left the courtroom having won the battle she'd come to win.

~

France

He had turned to the bottle, and Troy hated himself for every sip. Every morning, he promised himself he'd give it up.

But it was hard when everything he'd ever wanted was pulled out from under him violently and suddenly.

When he couldn't stop thinking about his girls, both of whom he'd been denied access to.

Eventually, he realized he must go on with life—but it felt shallow and empty.

How could he ever survive without his beautiful Della? His sweet Judy? The family they made together was perfect; how could he bear the brokenness?

One thing kept him going: the thought that, someday, Adele would be forced to return to him. She must. After all, she'd loved him, hadn't she?

And would a woman in love simply cease feeling what she'd assured him she felt? No. It couldn't be. Somewhere within, she still loved him.

He wouldn't accept this divorce. Yes, he'd been forced by man-made laws to sign documents saying they were divorced, but he didn't believe it, not in his heart. They were still married, and she would return because she must.

So Troy determined to wait her out, to keep on pretending that she would be back. That she'd drive up the long road to the house, step out, and walk up the steps. There he'd be, ready to pull her into his arms and smother apologies with kisses.

Yes, that was just how it'd be. And then he'd have his perfect family again.

With that in mind, he set to making the vineyard a place Adele would love to raise her children.

He did some minor puttering, a fresh coat of paint and hired a boy to fix the little garden at the back which his Della had deemed too tangled for even her to repair—and then he focused on the vineyard.

If he could make it profitable, perhaps wealth in a small way would influence Adele. Perhaps she'd see that he could support her, that he was working hard because he loved her not because he didn't want to be with her …

If only he could show her that all the lies that lawyer had spoken about his neglect and lack of concern for her feelings were just that—filthy lies.

But she knows that, doesn't she? asked his heart

in agony late at night. *She knows I love her. She must. I told her every day I was with her. More than once some days. She knows. She just … she's forgotten.*

Somehow, without seeing her, he must remind her. But he couldn't let her know it was all for her now—no. She must come to him of her own volition. She must love him for himself.

And then, only then, would they be a family again.

The ball was in her court; he would bide his time.

So pride held him away from a baby girl whom he loved from a distance. He tried to make it right by offering a shallow glimpse of fatherhood in way of regular checks, Christmas cards, and the occasional toy or trinket sent but oftentimes returned unopened.

In the meantime, he made friends, as he was always wont to do, and he talked to Holt a great deal, and rang his sister up when he felt particularly depressed—though he always pretended to be cheerful for her.

He didn't date again, let alone enter a serious relationship.

Other women had never been an option, anyway. There would never be another Della. He'd accepted that, and he knew he'd be waiting for her forever if that was how long it took.

And, as the spiral of life sucked him up, more than ever, he let his frail relationship with his Lord and Master fall away until it was nothing but a whispered prayer before bedtime like a nod toward an ancient Father whom he didn't really want to talk to.

~

Guilt was a feeling which Adele was only mildly familiar with. It struck hard as the months rolled by, and Troy said nothing save to keep sending the checks, the presents, that she always sent back.

Yet the agony of being parted from Judy—and from Adele—was reflected in the cryptic words Lola Cole spoke when she came to visit her look-alike niece.

Lola loved Judy, though she didn't drop by often. Adele suspected it was partially due to the fact that she'd broken an adored big brother's heart and, almost, she thought, a larger part due to the fact that a longed-for child had not blessed Dave and Lola Cole's nest.

Adele could understand jealousy, too, and she admired a woman who simply chose to remove the temptation to the ugly feeling from her life completely.

There were days when Adele wondered if she couldn't just give Judy to Lola. Eventually, that would mean that Troy got her, one way or another, and Troy deserved the baby; Adele didn't.

But she couldn't give Judy up. She just couldn't.

As the weeks passed, she threw herself more and more into the gay, carefree life, seeking to recapture her former self.

She starved down to nothing, applied loads of makeup, covered her arms, neck, and ears with jewelry, and flirted and drank until her mind, soul, and body all suffered heavily.

She didn't know why she did it—only that it helped a little, made her feel more like herself. Surely

Judy didn't mind being left with Millie! She was a bottle baby, and a quiet one at that, and Millie loved her adopted niece.

Adele returned to her work at the flower shop within a few weeks of arriving back in London, as the tenant's rent had run out. She could keep the baby with her, which pleased any woman who came in.

It took her a bit to figure out how to play Judy's presence with the men who'd formerly flirted with her as if she hadn't a care in the world—when plainly she now did—but she soon learned to rouse a protective instinct in them.

It took so little; men were inclined to protect women and babies, especially attractive women with babies who didn't mind being passed about and manhandled a bit, even if big blue eyes were wide with fright the whole time. Judy's shocked expression only increased their amusement.

Mother moved to London a few months after Adele's divorce was finalized. She didn't give a particular reason for selling her home of over thirty years and moving to a city she hated, but Adele came to a slow conclusion as the years past.

It was to be with Judy.

If Adele had been the bane of her mother's existence, Judy was the light of her life. Mother doted on her granddaughter, and in no time, she whisked Judy away from her mother for nights on end.

On the subject of her daughter's divorce, Adele's motherhood, and all aspects related to those two subjects, there began to be regular shouting matches between Mother and Adele.

Millie also spoke to Adele many times on the

subject of Mr. Troy Kee and his place in her life, as well as the neglect Judy was receiving for no apparent reason.

There were times when Millie and Adele's quarrels grew heated, but unlike with Mother, Adele pacified and cooed over Millie until each forgave the other and life moved on.

Yet even Millie stuck to her beliefs despite her puppy dog worship of her dynamic best friend. She would not be swayed by all Adele's whining arguments, made-up sob stories, and temperamental rants.

Adele soon learned two things. First, that leaving one's husband was an unpardonable sin, and if she hadn't been going to the hottest part of Hell before, she was now. Second, that if it weren't for Mother, Judy would be dead—and probably in Heaven.

Yet Adele wanted to be a good mother—really, she did. She just didn't have time to mind a tiny baby, and then a tiny toddler, and then a tiny child.

As the years went by, her love became more and more distant until she left Judy to herself most days—as well as far into the night.

She chased men more than ever before, even allowed her own standards to slip more than she would have before her marriage to Troy Kee.

She vaguely knew she was rebelling against something, and she told herself it was her husband's unrealistic expectations, but it wasn't that.

Adele was rebelling against Something greater than a man.

By the time she was three, Judy spent half her week with her beloved Granny and the other half being occasionally tended to by Auntie Millie, who by then had her own apartment. She was left to her own devices the rest of the time.

With big blue eyes and red-tinted blonde hair, Judy was going to be a beauty. Adele was proud of her, really. Thought she was a fine little girl.

Yet with every passing day, she felt these emotions more and more distantly as she allowed her fears and ghosts and selfishness to obliterate them. Yes, she loved Judy … but Judy could take care of herself.

So Judy became a Granny-raised child, and Adele pursued her own pleasure, her soul lost somewhere in the past.

~

She wished she had more people to snuggle with. There was just Granny and Auntie Millie, and neither of them were there near enough for all the snuggles one needed to get through the day.

She wished sometimes someone would say, "I love you," and that someone would be her mother.

She wished that the mysterious man whom her mother hated and her granny wanted to come back would show up and tell her he loved her, too.

But he couldn't love her, of course, because he wasn't there; one didn't love from France, wherever that was.

She wished she could watch her mother whisk about the room in her high heels and perfumed skirt, shiny earrings swinging, all day. Mother was so very pretty.

She wished Mother wouldn't bring home men. She didn't like them; she never had.

They were all so big and loud and scary. Sometimes they smelled funny, too.

Granny said that meant they'd been drinking, though she never said what they'd been drinking. Something that made them silly, she guessed.

She wished her mother was home some nights when bad dreams woke her up and left her sobbing softly, frightened of monsters under her bed or in her closet or hidden among the perpetual clutter that filled their small apartment.

She wished that when her mother was home, she would allow her to come to her room and sleep there, cuddled up next to her, and listen to her heartbeat until she fell asleep. She knew somehow that that would be the best kind of sleep.

And she waited. Because sometimes, when very small, one has to wait to be thought of.

That was all right. She'd learned to be the patient sort.

To Be Continued ...

The Kees & Colliers series will continue with book 2, *The Lady of the Vineyard.*

A Note to the Reader

Thank you so much for the time you took to read this novel! I write for you, so obviously I'm grateful for the time you gave to me. I hope you enjoyed this novel and will continue on to book 2 for more time with Troy, Adele, and of course little Judy.

I'm so excited to have finally released the final version of this novel. Though imperfect, I still love it, with all its little idiosyncrasies!

I wrote this novel in about two weeks, directly after the death of my beloved grandfather. It's more emotional and moody than any book I've written before or ever will write, fueled by my feelings of despair and in disarray. I felt like my own soul was astray—and this was the perfect story to write to sort out those complicated feelings.

I still miss my granddad. I still hate all the fallout that happened because of his death. I'm sad that my family will never be the same way again. I mourn for my lost childhood and innocence; I'm sorry for the mistakes I made and the sins I committed to forget.

But there is grace for my darkest places—and more than that, hope. Things do get better. If I could go back and hug little seventeen-year-old me and tell her one thing, it would be, "God is bigger than even this—and He loves you despite knowing you."

I related a lot to the song *God Only Knows* by For King & Country as God dragged me out of the fog. As the song states, "There's a kind of love that God only knows." No one else can reach you, help you, save you like Jesus Christ. I beg you, if you have ever doubted, to turn to Him, for He is so great and mighty!

That said, I never want to write a novel in which things are easy. I've read those kinds of books, and they're so shallow. The incredible truth about God is He meets us in the rubble of our lives. Leaving behind our sins, our trauma, and every other facet of our worldly pasts is not easy. However, it is possible—and where there is potential, there is, again, that brilliant hope.

I pray this novel blessed you, but if it didn't, no worries. Post a review either way! The negative ones help convince people that it isn't just my friends posting reviews. (They don't, by the way. For whatever reason, my dearest friends absolutely refuse to take the time. Ingrates.)

Also, we should connect! I'm on Instagram a lot (@kellynrothauthor) and I'm trying to figure out TikTok (same username, much more cringey), but I also have a newsletter I like to nudge people toward: https://kellynrothauthor.com/newsletter/

There just might be a free story in it for you. ;-)

God bless you & keep you—may He make His face shine upon you—may the Lord lift up His countenance upon You and give You peace.

Kellyn Roth
March 2022
White Salmon, WA

Made in the USA
Columbia, SC
20 April 2022